Bridgetown's Children

Bridgetown's Children

Adam Breindel

To Gryphonne

"More is different."
– Philip W. Anderson

In 1890, Robert Porter, Henry Gannett, and William Hunt reported for the Census Bureau on the "Progress of the Nation" in a document of the same name. The men declared that the nation had in fact so progressed that the American frontier no longer existed.

Because, in those days, they were counting men and not how those men behaved.

On some sheets of paper, Portland, Oregon might be a settled part of the United States of America and subject to all of the law that comes therewith. But nobody has yet succeeded in convincing the town's residents.

These were more or less my thoughts—and not for the first time—as I crawled out of a driving rain and collapsed face first onto a muddy floor constructed of fiberglass derelict boat hull.

I was inside a tangled mound of partial vessels, lashed together with stolen wire and tent lines, comprising a sort of half-floating public house. The entire assemblage was tied—for the moment—near the foot of the Ross Island Bridge.

I tried to pick up my head and throw the proprietor a grin. I had limited success and attempted a bad joke instead.

– The usual and ... can I borrow the doc?

I slumped back down.

A ruddy bearded man about forty-five knelt next to me and lifted my jacket as high as it would freely go.

– I can cut this off of you but it's a nice jacket.

– No, I'll try and ... damn, that arm isn't working. Ok ... Cut 'er off.

A seven-inch commando-style knife served as trauma shears. The pricey looted weapon was a contrast to the dollar-store flashlight shining in my eyes.

– I see two rounds. Deep in your back near the left shoulder blade. Probably not too bad.

– I heard three or four shots total, but he must've missed with a couple. Still hurt like hell.

– Yeah, it'll hurt even more getting them out. But luckily we have Portland's finest housemade painkillers for ya.

He meant fentanyl, titrated by the man himself to where he was pretty confident it wouldn't kill me. Smoked for fast onset and with a ready Narcan chaser in case his brew was off and it looked like I wasn't coming back.

I took a hit. The taste made my stomach heave for a second. I felt "Doctor" Eddie start poking my shoulder, and then the world slipped away.

When the house lights started coming up, at least I knew where I was: lying on a filthy soaking couch in a shack behind the bar, also made of boat hulls and illuminated with LED tree lights. It doubled as a stock room and so, although I couldn't quite move, I looked longingly at a line of stolen, factory-sealed fifths of New Amsterdam vodka. I tried levitating one with my mind.

The moldy stank of rotten foam rose through dog-chewed holes in the cushion under my head.

The "doc" came in smiling.

– That makes five bullets this year and it's barely even spring. You gotta stand your ground, start shooting back, brother. And get yourself some armor. I know a guy...

– Armor maybe... – I groaned – The rest ... you know how it works.

– I guess once they've killed you, you'll have earned a break from the man.

Hah. He had a point.

When I'm not running down insurance fraud or doing the expert witness dance for juries who can't count, I'm a private detective. Yeah, we still exist.

We're a flavor of armed rent-a-cop with just a slightly larger paycheck and a lot more opportunities to get in trouble. For now, the business is flourishing in Stumptown. Surprise, surprise: stubborn people with even a little money are willing to spend some of it to keep the rest. And when there are no cops to do the job, we're the next cheapest option.

But it's a paradoxical line of work. On one hand, business is good when things get sketchy. On the other, the gig only exists where folks are civilized enough to try looking for answers or working the system before resorting to violence of their own.

And so employment prospects here are perennially iffy. When victims don't see results and get sufficiently desperate, people like me are out on our asses and the real hard guys take over. I've been to places that got that way and stayed, and it's uglier for everyone. So I still nourish a self-serving hope that this town doesn't get all the way there.

I know what you might be thinking. Some people say that Portland is not only civilized but maybe too civilized: that we're soft—communists, even!—when they hear about the taxes and the social service slogans. But the pols are crooked, the taxes are bribes, and the services are smoke and mirrors with a side of snake oil. Which is to say, it's a good ol' corrupt American burg on the edge of the wilderness. Nothing more, nothing less.

Honestly, that suits me until the lead starts flying.

I get a touch philosophical when the drugs start wearing off but the pain hasn't yet made itself known. Let me calm down, back up about a week, and try to make some sense.

The Multnomah Hotel was put up when trains and steamboats convinced Portland timber barons that it was time to have a proper place to stay in town and that a buck could be made standing one up. If the grand pre-war cut stone structure was the crown of Portland, then the Yamhill Room, where I was currently downing gin, was the jewel.

At least it had been. These days, power players drank elsewhere and left the Yamhill to tourists who didn't notice stained brass, cracked leather, and a severely worn parquet (or at least didn't mind it) when they bellied up to the longest marble bar west of Chicago.

Manny Gil ran security for the property and the look he gave me as he strode in said it was time to earn the substantial discount I got on booze. Most frequently that meant brushing the bums out of the lobby. Otherwise, city hall gossip was currency.

Gossip wouldn't cover the tab tonight. Per Manny, just moments before, someone had made off with a guest's laptop bag from the hotel restaurant. It looked like the thief might have known what he was looking for and, unless he had a getaway car waiting, he couldn't be more than two blocks away. He had exited the lobby by the east doors and was last seen heading for the river.

I gave Manny a look. The odds were really slim on this. He shook his head, I swigged the last of my glass, and a few seconds later found myself sprinting down SW Ash.

I saw a plausible suspect and bag entering the riverfront park. If I was lucky, the thief had been held up by cars trying to cross Naito and this was the guy.

He turned north and diagonalled across the park toward the river. I was racing and sweating but easily fifty yards back. He turned farther north.

The thought was just crystalizing in my mind that this was a really strange way to try and flee when someone rather heavier than my one hundred seventy pounds slammed into me from the side and took me to the grass in a football tackle. I flipped over and slammed a hand into his throat before he could consolidate his position on top of me. I squirmed out. Even if I didn't have the strength I once had as a high school wrestler, I kept the approximate build and reflexes. I popped up, saw him alone and still lying on the ground clutching his throat, and kept running toward the river.

I made it fifty more yards when something like a pipe hit the back of my head and I felt wet concrete and then nothing.

When the world slowly came back, I was lying in the grass, my head throbbing but otherwise intact.

I had everything I started the evening with, including wallet, phone, and gun. So there was that. But the bag and everyone associated were long gone.

Sometimes this is how it goes, I thought, as I pulled myself together to share the bad news. I stumbled up and leaned into a sloppy jog back toward the Multnomah. Manny was watching serenely while front desk staff gently argued with a frantic guest in a corduroy suit. I caught his eye and headed to the corner of the lobby.

– I missed the real action, didn't I?

– How did you know?

– I got halfway to the bridge chasing the guy when his buddy jumped me. Got away from him and got beaned in the skull by another.

I reached up and felt the lump on my head.

– Would have been an unlikely coincidence to begin with, but when I came to and realized I hadn't been robbed or even relieved of my piece, I knew it was a setup. So what did I miss?

– The whole thing was an odd grab and run. Another guy—I guess a third man? fourth man?—takes this other gentleman's laptop bag in the bar. But here's the weird thing. He dumps it on the ground, pokes around the mess of cables alongside a brand new laptop—the guy says it cost five thousand dollars—and then takes off with just the empty bag. Guy here claims there were irreplaceable documents in the bag. But that means the thief knew enough to leave the computer and bolt, so it couldn't have been random.

– Not to mention – I added – a third or fourth player on the visiting team is super unusual for this kind of operation. There were some logistics and planning involved—more than the average crook is accustomed to trying.

– Yeah that's pretty much unheard of around here. Our clientele just isn't classy enough to deserve actual planned crime.

He gave a wry smile.

Manny Gil was a bit atypical for the hotel security boss job, having never worked as a cop, a detective, a soldier, or even a security guard. He'd grown up in East Providence, Rhode Island, son of Azorean immigrants who taught him fishing, winemaking, and carpentry, somewhat against his will. As soon as he finished high school, he bailed on New England and headed for the Pacific Northwest grunge scene where his band, Manny and the Gillfish, played a couple years of local shows before fizzling out. Though he didn't hit it big as a musician, his height and calm assertiveness got him from part-time bouncer to running club security and then to head of security ops for decent-sized music festivals. In that world, it didn't hurt that he was an artist and not a cop.

I met him in his festival days and he had always maintained the "we're all here to have fun but we're not gonna have any nonsense" vibe. That approach turned out to be the perfect one for a Portland hotel, where security needed to stay low key and soft power solved more problems than a cop's taser. The festival mindset was also handy where narcing was a lot less important than keeping people alive—guests or homeless alike—when they inevitably OD'd on the property.

A burning tingle at the base of my skull on the left side took hold of my attention. I felt it and it was oozing something warm and sticky. They had hit me harder than I'd realized.

– You should get that looked at. We have a paramedic in house for the conference and she's bored to death...

– Don't worry about that. Just bummed this one got away.

The bar was nearly empty now and Manny disappeared momentarily, returning with a sizable pour of Japanese whisky.

– Get some sleep. Maybe it's nothing. We'll find out more tomorrow if the guests do all of the police and insurance paperwork.

I walked the seven blocks to my apartment building, an unremarkable low-rise near the west edge of Chinatown, and dragged myself upstairs and inside. I'd apparently left all the lights on since morning. I cursed, dumped my clothes and gear on the bed, and stumbled into a hot shower.

After cleaning up a bit, I lay down and thought briefly about pouring another drink. Before I could act on the impulse, I was out.

3

I woke up to the noise of a delivery truck lift gate next door and the shouts of the crew resupplying the corner store. That meant it was ... a bit after eight already. I felt mostly functional and decided to chat with Manny and then swing by the office.

The Multnomah was buzzing with guests when I arrived, conference goers at some event to do with urban design. Manny wouldn't be in until nine-thirty, so I killed the time lurking in talks about historical cronyism and building permits in the vicinity of some now-disused rail yards.

It was more interesting than I'd anticipated, but I was quickly lost in the minutiae of academic detail at the intersection of building codes, design, and political hagiography debates.

My eyelids were closing when a hand clasped my shoulder and another waved a cappuccino under my nose. Manny grinned and motioned for me to follow.

His outfit—vastly oversized black T-shirt, black jeans, and Doc Martens—hadn't changed since I'd first met him and it was usually perfect camouflage in town. Not today. The guests were to a person overdressed for the locale in elbow patch academic cliche.

We sat together in the security office squinting at digital playback from the night before.

– Anything?

– Not really. It does seem like more than a usual grab-and-run, but I can't see the why. How's the head anyway?

– Thanks for looking. Head? Good as new. Amateurs.

– That's good. Go by the bar. Take another cap with you to the office.

The fog and cold drizzle refreshed me on the short walk. Portland's Old Town is home to a variety of beautiful stone buildings, with commercial space on the ground floor and office space above. Absent demand for those, most of the space stays empty. The buildings don't meet seismic code for housing, and compassionate lawmaking prefers people dying out on the streets today over possibly dying indoors in a potential earthquake. For obscure real estate accounting reasons, as office space it's still over my budget. So I'm in a less glamorous spot across Burnside over a dispensary.

I continued puzzling over the three-card-monte bag grab as I got my mail from the box, drifted into the elevator, and rode up to the second floor. Some days, the stairs were my only exercise and my doctor warned me to avoid them at my peril. No matter. Today I was riding. And, anyway, I had plenty of peril coming my direction. I shuffled out of the elevator.

I was alternately sorting paperwork, procrastinating by paying bills on my phone, and dozing, when I got a notification that I'd missed a call and had a voicemail waiting.

I almost unlocked the phone. For some reason, I just didn't have the energy. I dozed off again.

The next time, the phone was more insistent.

First message was noise and a hangup. Second message was from ex-commissioner Samuel Bain, a well meaning and only mildly crooked character to whom I was warm on a professional basis. Opportunities for embarrassment come thick in politics and all the successful players kept small teams of poorly paid investigators for continuous bomb-defusing and mine-clearing runs. The work was predictable. And, beyond the cash, I appreciated the chance to fill out my own roster of support for the inevitable brushes with authority that my work entails.

"Do you remember Rick San Roman? He keeps a low profile but he's an important donor and he needs to chat with you about an urgent matter. If you're caught up on the news, you might already have a guess where this is going. If not, take a look and then grab a taxi up to the San Roman place. He's on the same street as my boss but a little farther up—1816. If you haven't seen his house, it's a trip—there's staff, there's family that don't always get along, there's guests squatting and stirring the pot. Can be a little unpredictable so don't let anything hang out. Thanks. I owe you another one."

I slurped a glass of water and opened a few apps to acquire situational awareness. It appeared I had slept through more of Portland weird than suited. In sum, today was the opening day of a global conference on distributed urban design, architecture, climate, and political diversity—an ultra narrow intersection where Portland played the role that Milan did for fashion. By some genius foresight—or dumb luck—this work was turning out to be critical for keeping the world running in the twenty-first century and the town was well placed to trade hard-earned learnings for foreign dollars. The low-budget academic hangers on made up the crowd at the Multnomah, while the real movers were at the Ritz Carlton.

One of those players, decorated architect and artistic tastemaker Ara San Roman, had been clubbed halfway to death waiting for the streetcar just outside the $600 million real estate jewel that housed the Ritz hotel and hosted several of the more exclusive conference events.

The paper neglected to add that Ricardo San Roman was Ara's adoptive father, and, over the decades, both a protégée of her grandfather and romantically involved with her mother.

I didn't like getting called in here. This case was the job of a big-city police department. The reader may know that Portland lacked one of those. And that the public scrutiny under which the threadbare police bureau worked meant that for certain kinds of cases, they couldn't be effective. Poor people turned to neighborhood "mayors" or enforcers; rich people to lawyers and investigators, at least to start.

Today's request, though, was too high profile for my comfort—notwithstanding San Roman's unquestionable ability to pay. Something was off and somebody—somebodies, likely—were going to get hurt. Meh ... maybe it's just Wednesday, I thought, pouring the rest of the glass of water into the window plant and opening my safe to grab some gear.

4

The rideshare from Old Town out to the upper part of Goose Hollow only took about ten minutes but out the window we crossed a continent and climbed a mountain at the same time.

Old Town, where we'd started and close to the river, had mixed the getting-it-done with the down-and-out—while catering to the down and out—since Portland was settled. Single men were as likely then as now to earn a bit, spend what they had, and promptly land in the gutter. Then it was logging, sailing, booze, gambling, and whoring. Now it was odd jobs, day labor, better booze, and fentanyl. Charities, churches, chippies and charlatans set up shop to address the market.

From there, we drove through half a dozen neighborhoods to arrive on San Roman's street on the near side of the hills. While the area featured massive houses and old money families, the blocks sloped toward downtown, to the river and the Cascade Range, the orchestra and historical society and Pioneer Courthouse Square. When their residents left home—even if they had drivers—they saw the reality of the city along their way. And that proximity now divided them from their brethren over the ridge or across the Willamette more than money, standing, or ancestry.

When the city burned and blocks were overrun by thieves, vandals, and fentanyl zombies, one side of the river mourned and fought while the other shopped and mumbled, in an embarrassed whisper, that they wouldn't ride the MAX alone or let their children go to PSU but there was nothing for it: justice demanded leaving the city to its fate.

Me, I'd take the Bains and the San Romans, warts and all, any day of the week.

My driver coughed to get my attention.

– This is it. Well, the app says this is it. Pull up to the gate?

– No, this is good. Thanks.

I handed him a generous tip.

– Everybody likes cash, right?

– You got that right.

I thanked him again, closed the door, and stepped away from the car. I couldn't see anything from the street. The flagged driveway disappeared into the wet gloom. The gate was ajar and I started through. If Mr. Ricardo San Roman wanted to keep tabs on the entrance, and I suspect he did, there would be infrared cameras on me. I didn't know where. I looked low into the trees, smiled, waved, and walked up the drive.

The house was a monstrous Tudor pile, based on the illuminated fraction I could see. The lawn and gardens, shrouded in shadow, were large enough that I heard crickets as I walked up fifty yards of driveway. As I approached the house, a light blinked on in a porte-cochere and a uniformed man emerged from a booth. This was something from another era. But then, time itself doesn't run the same way around here.

– Please accept my apologies for the walk in the dark. Mr. San Roman did not expect you on foot. This way, please.

We walked into a paneled foyer.

– Can I offer you a drink?

He stepped behind a counter and his hands came up with a tray containing a bottle of sparkling water, a glass of ice, a lemon, and—I realized only when he handed it to me—a refrigerated towel.

– Thanks. I'm ready just as soon as Mr. San Roman is.

The butler disappeared. A minute passed. Then two. A door slid open somewhere behind me and I turned.

A very large man—taller than me by the better part of a foot and twice as wide, with waves of silver hair, in a pine green suit the likes of which hadn't been seen outside gag parties and disco nights in fifty years—unceremoniously harrumphed into the room. He stretched his hand toward me.

– Apologies for the circus. I appreciate your coming on short notice.

I didn't know what he was talking about, but said nothing.

– Let's talk in my office.

We stepped into a tiny elevator which instantly filled with his cologne. He drove us upward by means of an antique brass toggle switch. About twenty-five seconds later the elevator jolted to a stop. We stepped out into the sort of traditional office suggested by the external architecture and the butler. I had no doubt that the view on a clear day would be impressive. At present, the entire room was dim, the principal light coming from a banker's lamp on San Roman's desk.

He motioned to two chairs and immediately collapsed into one. There was no further ceremony. He didn't even look at the decanter on the sideboard.

– You're up to date on what happened to my daughter?

– I figured that must be the trouble. But why me? Aren't the cops, the sheriff, the OSP, and a couple of private outfits all over this? Especially with artists, policy people, and bigwigs visiting town...?

– Not them yet. This is too personal for me.

– Think it has anything to do with that guy you and Ara's grandfather put away, big operations guy in the 90s heroin scene or something like that? Maybe...

– You mean the one with the osprey tattoo they called Magenta? No, that was finished a million years ago. He'd be way past his prime now anyway.

– Sorry to be blunt, but how do you know? Isn't that how Ara's parents...?

– Please stop. You don't know what you're talking about. Ara's parents died in a car crash on I-5, middle of nowhere. Tragic, but there was no one else involved. Now, listen to me. I've already seen a bunch of security camera footage. Before the cops even saw it...

My eyes went up but he shushed me with his hand.

– ...and it's one of these drugged-out nuts. They'll never catch him unless he turns up dead in a tent. I need you to get to him before that.

Anger, fear, and sorrow do crazy things to people but San Roman ought to know better. His story made it sound like a random attack. Rough, but random. And the guy was probably so far out of his mind that he had no idea what he was even doing. The system couldn't do much of anything with the guy even if we caught him. What was the point?

Then again, this was an opportunity to keep my initial thoughts to myself. I had to get some more info and buy a little time. This was a loser and yet an offer I might not be able to refuse.

– Can we ... take a look at any of the video? See what we have to work with?

San Roman slowly let out his breath and his face softened.

– Yes. Yes. I feel better already. Just knowing you're on my team. Here, I've got two different angles.

He pulled out a laptop, flipped it around and played the gruesome attack in high definition. Three times from each of the two angles.

The assailant, by behavior, did resemble downtown's classic drug-addled or mentally ill street dwellers. A hoodie, a sloppy unusual gait, sudden jerking movements, the production of a bottle, waving it to the side, up, back, and then ... the brutal pummeling. Ara was probably lucky the heavy glass didn't break partway through the assault. If you could use the word lucky at all in a case like this.

– That's some clear film but you know the deal ... either the cops already know who this is, in which case they're a mile ahead of us, or, if they don't, they'll be scouring the usual hangouts before I get there. Even more likely, this nut goes to ground and we're all in the dark. You know this isn't just personal. It's a political shitshow. With the conference, we're on the front pages in London, Berlin, and Singapore again for all the wrong reasons. Everyone will be running around trying to look like they're taking some useful action.

– Yes ... but no matter what happens, in this town, they tend to walk. As long as Ara is alive, this character won't see the inside of a cell. And I need to ... have a private discussion with him before he disappears.

– I get it, but this puts me in an awkward spot. What you're suggesting is a little too far and you know it. And if you don't know that then ... well I don't want to know. On the other hand it seems we all owe things to each other and so we're riding this damned bus together. I'll take a little look but that's all for now.

He wasn't happy but he was a skilled negotiator. He accepted the concession.

– Anything else you can give me? Is Ara awake? Can you send me those images?

– No, no, and already done. Please just get started.

He gestured toward the elevator and I started walking. Before I got to its odd closet-like door, I sensed San Roman right behind me then felt his hand on my shoulder.

– Look. I'm really not like that. Well, not entirely like that. The thing is, you're right about how we all owe things to each other. And taking care of this is something I owe to Ara's mother.

He glanced down. He was holding the framed five-by-seven whose back I had been staring at on his desk. The obverse bore a glamorous grande dame with a notable resemblance to Ara.

Was he choking up?

– I get it.

I entered the elevator. I might have seen a tear before the door completely closed.

5

I had some thinking to do and I didn't trust myself at home or in the office due to the presence of substantial quantities of alcohol. So I headed for the Sedgewick Hotel, which also possessed quantities of alcohol but where I wasn't in a position to partake. I helped them out with security and they let me drink coffee and think but not drink. They were "new school" and didn't appreciate the effect of gin on problem solving or foot pursuits.

I nursed a black coffee, doodled on an actual paper notepad, and wondered how the hell I had gotten into any of this. Although none of it had made any sense at the time, in retrospect my career almost looks plausible if you close one eye and squint.

I started out as a math guy and for work found myself looking at insurance claims. I quickly learned a lot about statistics and the real world not covered in school. There are three kinds of insurance fraud investigations: the ones looking for any excuse to deny payment, regardless of circumstances and likelihoods; the ones examining routine amateur con artistry of inexperienced people lying or stretching the truth; and the big ones, the ones where the stakes were grander than a number in an insurance company spreadsheet. In those cases, lives and livelihoods truly were on the line: arsons impacted dozens of families or hundreds of workers; malefactors earned long prison terms; massive construction disasters left unmistakable evidence of foul play.

I was assigned to the first kind of investigation until I got sick of myself for doing it; the second kind until I learned enough that I was sick of the job and could do it without trying; and the third kind until I got frustrated aiming at quiet settlements when I wanted to try and address, at least a little, the rough-edged reality of the world.

There are people interested in that reality and some are even willing to pay. They rarely have insurance-scale money, though. I guess the statistical term would be survivorship bias: folks end up with a lot of dough by not worrying too much about reality when they can agree on a settled fiction for less.

Ricardo San Roman might be an exception or he might not. I had heard a lot of things and I wasn't sure which ones to believe.

After a couple of hours of contemplation and observation, the coffee was getting to my stomach. The hotel restaurant wouldn't be open for a few more hours and anyway I wasn't about to pay their prices before I felt like I had enough of a handle on the case to start billing.

I went across the street and began walking south for a late lunch at a spot that started out as hipster retro showpiece but then, as the hipsters left and reality sank in, morphed into a halfway legit west coast diner.

It was not a good afternoon downtown. The streets were something out of Les Miserables, with fetty in place of wine. The only Marius around proclaiming a dream of rallying the downtrodden was a bald smug hipster running for city council. His slogans, snark, and thick rimmed glasses shone from a billboard. But the "people's candidate" was too busy pandering to rebellious Reed kids to come across the river and see the man in front of me, a seventy-year-old with wisps of white hair, passed out against the curb, starving to death because he had no teeth.

All the while, inside the diner, past cracked and double boarded glass doors, Monseigneur's bourgeois successors could get their chocolate prepared in as fancy a manner as they might like. My wandering rumination gave way to perplexity when I found Tara, the diner's owner, working the counter in a blouse, skirt, and suit jacket.

– Why the fancy business outfit?

– Fresh off a TV appearance!

– What are you doing on TV?

– It turns out that this building was one of the first "green" buildings in North America—maybe the world—built to match an early-twentieth-century design. With the Europeans and everyone here for the conference, someone at channel six thought it might be fun to see how a place that looks like this...

She gestured at the art deco windows and the entryway that ran parallel to her store, from the street straight through to elevators and concierge desk, following a pattern rarely seen anymore.

– ...can manage to be sexy, green, and cheap all at the same time.

– And yours was the best-looking face on the first floor...

– Just the only one here today and happy to grab some free promotion. Gotta hustle.

I found myself smiling, almost laughing. I ordered a turkey club and scrolled through my phone. Skimming the news, it appeared someone's PR plan was coming together: despite the grime, crime, and crooked pols, the city was back on the (inside section) front pages of capitals around the world combining sustainable quirky success, bleeding-edge architecture and transit, with salmon in the river and wolves on Mt. Hood.

Maybe it was the sandwich working miracles on my mood or Tara's cute country-girl-in-the-city look. Either way, I started feeling increasingly up to the job. I stood, stretched, rifled through my bag, a nervous habit ostensibly ensuring nothing had gone missing. I thanked Tara and turned for the door to the inside passage, where I glanced upward to enjoy a quick dose of art deco thrill.

All of the shiny news coverage in the world wasn't going to get Ara's attacker off the streets or into San Roman's grasp. I had some work to do, starting with spending more time squinting at video of the attack.

I left the building and headed to my office which, unlike my last stop, was of a genuine early-twentieth-century vintage and lacked any of the architectural glamor, eco-friendly engineering, and functioning climate control that Tara's diner enjoyed.

My thoughts were unfocused, drifting, my eyes just barely skimming my surroundings as I walked up to the building and pulled the electronic door key out of my pocket. Before I could bring it to the doorframe, I caught a sense of aggressive movement to my right. Reflexively, I stepped and turned so my back was covered by the vestibule and I could face any potential threat head on.

Something didn't quite add up and I froze. And that half second is all it took for a thin ginger girl with a pixie and a leather jacket to barrel into me at about fifteen miles per hour. She weighed maybe ninety pounds and barely rocked me back on my heels.

She bounced off of me and against the opposite side of the entry vestibule while I looked down for blood. A sharp knife can get a good part of the way to killing you without your feeling a thing. Looking for red is more reliable than seeing if anything hurts, but even a serious stab wound can take some time to bleed through clothing.

I could afford 500 milliseconds to assess before reacting. The girl didn't look aggressive; she looked terrified. Was she crazy? High? Was a second attack coming? No sign yet. And no evidence of a weapon, proper or improvised.

It sounds absurd to say that I took a risk putting my hand on her shoulder and moving out of a defensive posture. In this era, and this part of town, let's leave it at less absurd than it sounds.

The girl pulled closer, huddled against me. Zippers, pins, and studs on her leather jacket pressed into my chest. She kept twisting her head, gaze feverishly sweeping the street. She spoke in a hoarse whisper.

– They're trying to kill me. They're fucking insane! You have to help me.

I looked at the empty street.

– Hmm... I think we're ok for now. Do you want to come inside? There's coffee and water in my office.

There was booze too, which I started to consider but, under the circumstances, I thought it best to limit the menu on offer.

– Yes. Pleeeease. Inside.

She was still scanning the street as I opened the door and led her in. I checked that both vestibule doors were locked on the off chance someone really meant business with her and, now, possibly, with me.

We rode the elevator up in silence and she floated warily behind me down the hall and into my office. I made an extra show of securing the door and turning two kinds of deadbolts.

– I think we'll be ok in here.

I wasn't sure if she was high and paranoid. Although I thought that was the most likely possibility, I couldn't help my curiosity. I handed her a bottle of water and she calmed down substantially as she sipped it.

– Can you tell me some more?

– So these gangster-looking guys in a purple Dodge Charger started following me. At first, I was like, fuck off. It happens all the time. I ignored them and turned down one-way streets so they'd give up. But they kept showing up. They'd race around the block or something. And then after a few minutes they just started following me against the traffic. Sucks for me, there is no traffic around here this time of day to stop them. They kept calling me over. Said they had something important to discuss. Showed me a gun. Didn't make much of an impression. I've seen plenty of guns.

Just when I was wondering where the tough-girl act was going to meet with the reality sitting in front of me, she cracked and started crying.

– I've seen 'em you know but they started shooting at me. Like actually shooting. I didn't even realize what was happening until I saw a window shatter. I started running as fast as I could. They followed and took another shot or two. They yelled and then I turned the corner to where you were and I guess they're gone?

– Now ... why would some "gangster-looking guys" be chasing you around, driving against traffic and shooting in broad daylight? What did you do to them?

I stepped back and gave her a good head to toe. The retro punk clothes were a stereotype but the fiery hair and—for the street urchin I took this girl to be—shiny clean skin were in no way common.

– And don't try to tell me they must have mistaken you for someone else. There aren't a lot of someone elses with your ... look ... bumming around these blocks.

– I swear I don't know. But whatever it is, they mean business. You have to help me.

– Do you have someplace you can go?

– Some friends in southwest. Can you ... like I guess if you can just get me onto a bus before they come back, then I'll be ok.

– That I can do. Which...

She pulled out a surprisingly shiny phone given my priors.

– Please just get me to Fifth and Burnside, and please please wait for the bus, it'll just be a few minutes. Then you can forget all about me.

Something was off here. No, multiple things were off. But the picture wasn't coming into focus for me yet. Habit kicked in and I tried to gather some intel.

– Sure. Let's walk down to the bus. Here's my card, by the way, you can put it in your phone...

– Ok, I'll text you, then I'll have it and you'll have my number in case ... something ... happens.

That was too easy.

– And your name is?

– Lauren

– Lauren...

I hoped she'd offer a last name, even though I knew it would almost certainly be fake. Anyway, she didn't offer.

We got halfway to Fifth and Burnside and I was musing on the likelihood that no threatening Dodge Charger actually existed ... when a Dodge Charger rounded the corner and the back seat passenger rolled down a tinted window. I saw part of a face, sunglasses, and blued steel.

A voice ripped out from that back seat.

– We're not fucking around, little girl. Get over here or I'll come and bring you here.

I turned to Lauren, pointed north, up Third Avenue, behind me.

– Run! Now!

She hesitated for just a moment. The Charger's tires squealed and slid as the driver swung the car away from the curb and then hopped it. Both rear doors swung open.

I looked back and pointed sharply again.

– Go!

Now she started sprinting. She had a twenty yard head start on two thugs from the Charger. They were dressed in the stereotypical leisurewear: tracksuits, pricey shoes, designer streetwear t-shirts, ball caps, and differed only in race and height. One was white and over six-foot-two, the other Black and closer to five-ten.

They both raised semiautomatics but didn't fire as they leaped in her direction.

There are a lot fewer legitimate, hard-core gangsters in this town than people think. Fewer even than the gangsters think. So I took a chance and dove in front of the tall white guy's legs. The move worked better than I had hoped; he tried to sidestep and jump but he was too late and went down flipping onto his side. The automatic escaped his grip and skittered to the middle of the road. The Black dude didn't break stride but kept after Lauren.

The man I had taken down was scrambling after his gun while I tried to immobilize him but I had the raw end of the deal with his feet in my face. When I righted myself he was already up and swung his weapon around to target me. Time slowed down and I saw the muscles in his hand start to clench when my own hasty shot went off, catching his right shoulder solidly with an expanding round. I followed it up with two more shots, which both missed because he had already started turning before I fired. I let him finish his trip to the pavement in peace. It wouldn't kill but would hurt like hell for a long time. I took a deep breath and shot forty seconds of 360-degree video—a lot longer than it feels like in the moment—catching the Charger squealing away backwards then disappearing to the west, used a plastic bag to grab the weapon he had dropped, put it in my backpack, and headed in the direction Lauren and her pursuer had gone.

I ran north at full speed, admittedly at my age not the speed it should be for this kind of work, for a good three minutes. Made it almost to the old post office building near the train station before I gave up.

I still didn't know what this was all about, but it appeared the girl was in more than a bit of trouble and had made some motivated enemies.

Without a lot of options—let alone a connection between Lauren, the thug I had just shot, and any paying work—I had to turn to the cops. The Portland Police Bureau wouldn't have much sympathy for the dude who aimed his 9mm at my face. At the same time, the wrong money had rented the DAs office. That meant if I wasn't lucky, my PI license, insurance examiner and handgun licenses were all little more than cheap pieces of plastic. It also meant my ass might be headed for at least a brief spell in the can.

6

I phoned Sgt. Berkson, a friend in the bureau and a solid cop, as I walked back to the scene. Then I called my criminal attorney. Don't get the wrong idea. No matter how many Dashiell Hammett stories you've read, lawyering up applies equally to investigators. By the time I got to the pool of blood, the navy Rose City Interceptor Explorers were already there, emergency lights flashing in the gathering darkness, but the guy who had tried to gun me down was long gone. Berkson came right up to me.

– You'll want this.

I handed him the guy's Glock.

– What did you use?

I lifted my shirt and let him grab a subcompact .380 out of its holster. He reflexively unloaded it, grabbed the ejected round from the pavement, looked it all over, and handed it back to me.

– You're lucky this guy took off. No victim and no witnesses, our movie star in the prosecutor's office will have to find someone else to hassle.

– Victim my ass. Movie star my ass.

He laughed momentarily, then turned serious again.

– Well, it is what it is around this town, at least for now. Still got the same lawyer? Have him bring in your statement and videos. Get everything filled in and dated now, just to cover yourself. Somehow I don't think your guy is gonna show up and make a complaint.

– Thanks, man... So you know anything about a purple Charger, serious but amateur bangers riding with a driver?

– Could be a lot of people... But you don't see that downtown a whole lot. And never chasing a little white girl. You said she was little and white?

– She was unusual. Looked like she could've been homeless, a runaway, maybe trafficked or just turning tricks, helping with the drug trade. That was at first. But she cleaned up a tiny bit and started looking more like a Catlin-Gable kid on the outs with her parents. The really interesting part was how quickly and naturally she did it, like second nature. That thing they call "code switching." It's like a perfect disguise, or natural disguise, or something like that. But here's the thing: it's not like acting—you can't learn any part—it only works with characters you've actually been.

– So you're telling me you ran into a prep school rebel slumming it in Old Town, who got herself in over her head with somebody. I wish I could say you're crazy but it happens once a month, easy. Now the gangland style response—that's something you don't see very often. There's really just no one in this area who operates that way.

– Can you track the car on the traffic cams?

– Technically yeah, but it'll take some time. Once I get the data into the system about the shooting, that'll unlock a few things. If she's a minor, that will help too. You think she was minor, right? Right. I'll call you.

– What about Six-Three-Juliet? Any chance from the air?

Sgt. Berkson laughed so hard he started to cough.

– I don't think so, but I love your can-do attitude, man! Go home. You shot someone. Think about your priorities in life.

I waved as he walked back to one of the SUVs.

7

I took Berkson's advice and headed home.

Mindlessly flipping through junk mail and pacing my small living room-kitchen combination, I was plagued by an unsettling nervous energy. At first, I told myself it was the violent encounter, but it became increasingly clear the problem was Lauren. No matter how much everything else might be a coincidence, there had to be some reason she had headed to my office in the first place.

The room was stuffy. Humid. Unusual for Portland. The A/C was taking a personal day so I opened the window and turned on a box fan. I stared at my spider plant. Turned. What the heck was the deal with Lauren?

It's like I'd seen her before somewhere, but, of course, I hadn't.

I reached for the gin my PCP told me to lay off of. That advice makes sense for them, right? I mean, his outfit is in the insurance business as much as the doctor business. And the insurance guy in me knows how they're running the stats. But I wasn't doing insurance or stats so much anymore.

Insurance and crime have strange entanglements before you even get to doing a deed. Insurance rents you a little piece of other people's lives and keeps you off the street from fucking up your own. At least where money is concerned. Disasters stemming from love or ambition are harder to average out and sell in pieces.

It's not generally legal to get insurance that covers you if you commit a crime. But, if it were, the numbers on those policies would be a hell of a read. The insurance guys are allowed to run their world on correlations because it's the only thing they have before the fact. A woman gets killed, her boyfriend or husband killed her more than a third of the time. Being the boyfriend didn't cause him to kill her. And picking a random boyfriend isn't likely to turn up a killer. But I'd charge a lot more for the policy on the dude. Sounds crazy but you can see it in action: it's why insurance that covers suicide costs more for men.

It's a cliche that "correlation isn't causation." But it's also a cop-out: no one gives a damn about anything except causation. We want to know what causes a guy to get blind drunk, strangle his girlfriend, blackmail the boss, fuck the mayor's wife, stab a guy for $6.50 and a TriMet card, or use a revolver to settle an argument.

Or attack a famous architect and beat her bloody in broad daylight.

And it turns out, just the way this universe is built, there's no way to figure out causes without bringing some outside knowledge to the matter at hand. It's like God wanted to guarantee an income for detectives.

Despite that divine beneficence, I was two months behind on rent (but not worried: in Portland, I'd die here and they probably still couldn't evict my corpse); a month behind on the Internet (a bit less forgiving). I had to manage priorities. Online records databases, coffee, and the tax man got my money first. Everyone else including Fred Meyer had to fight for what was left. I pushed all the bills into my top drawer and slid it shut.

None of this was shedding any light on the San Roman case or on Lauren. Although... I wondered what she would look like a bit older. I flipped open my laptop and asked AI for some help. I'd need a photo. For lots of reasons my office is usually recording video, so I downloaded a still and tossed it into the maelstrom of matrices that manufactured images in the cloud.

8

I was unlocking the front building door at my office the following morning when a tall, thin man, nervous and suspiciously well dressed for the Pacific Northwest strode up, called out, "Mr. Louis"—without pronouncing the "s"—and reached to shake my hand. He had on a light overcoat, open to reveal a suit that didn't look cheap. It's hard to find one of those here outside a courtroom so I naturally assumed he was of the legal profession.

It also seemed odd to be, for the second time in as many days, greeted on my way into the office by someone who apparently had been looking for me and aiming to meet outside of the customary appointment model.

– Weatherson. Dr. Chuck Weatherson. Glad I found you here today. Do you have a moment, Jacques, er, Mr. Louis?

Jacques. And again without the "s." Gotta nip this in the bud.

– It's Jack. Jack Louis. (Hard "s.") At least on this side of the Atlantic and south of the forty-ninth... Anyway, ok, let's go upstairs.

I gestured toward the inside of the building.

It took a lot of emotional control to minimize the snark

– You're welcome to call, email, or text me and schedule an appointment anytime you need to. No need to stand out here in the street.

– Yes. Well. Thank you. I. This came up a bit urgently.

– For better or worse, matters in my work usually do.

He laughed once then turned grave again.

– Yes, that must be true. I am … that is, I was … chief of surgery, transplants at Emanuel Medical Center in Seattle. I have my own clinic now…

He hurried to explain as we shuffled through the narrow door to my office. I sat at my desk while he paced nervously.

– Ok, what brings you to an investigator in Portland, Dr. Weatherson?

– It's somewhat a matter of finances. Collections. You know, just tracking down an unpaid bill really…

– I see. Well, there are big, well organized firms that can help with that. It's really a whole industry. There's not too much I could probably do unless – I joked – the patient is here in town ready to pay and just can't find your address.

He was not amused.

– It's a bit complicated. The patient's … uhm … financially responsible party is … I suspect … here in town. I think she … they … don't understand how important it is to settle up.

– Well, doc. So … it's pretty unusual for someone with means not to understand the concept of payment for services … or do you mean they are pursuing bankruptcy to evade the debt? Like it or not, they have rights under the law. They can do that.

– They're not...

He stopped.

– Or do you suspect they have the money and are planning to orchestrate a bankruptcy? If that's the case, then there is a chance I could find some helpful evidence for an eventual court proceeding. But I need to be honest: I'm involved in another case right now and this is at the very periphery of my expertise. I can track people and I'm an old hand at the insurance game ... but if we're talking sophisticated finance schemes, I know a guy who's a genius with forensic accounting and –

He cut me off.

– No, I need your help with this. It's a ... a bit like what you said but not quite on the ... in the ... way where normal legal avenues will be available to them or to me.

– Ok, wait. Before we go any further, I'm up on all the gender pronoun stuff going around but why did you say "she" first and then "they"?

– I'm sorry. I'm really not any good at this. I'm a surgeon not ... well ... I'm a damned good surgeon and I should have stuck with that. Things have gotten complicated. The party is a woman. A girl, really. I wasn't sure how much I should say. The point is I need to find her. I'm ninety-nine percent sure she's here in Portland. And I need to get the money.

– Well, first of all, the most I could do is find out about this young woman and her finances. The rest is up to the courts if she doesn't want to pay. Like I said, there's a whole industry...

– Ok, let's ... let's take it one step at a time. Can I pay you to find her? Just that much. Ten thousand dollars for forty-eight hours if you can try and turn her up and contact me at the Nines. It's my hotel. It's over by the Pioneer Courthouse, the main lobby is up on –

I interrupted.

– Yes, I know. Great place. Go on.

– The girl goes by Jessica. She looks like this – he handed me two photos – and she'll be hanging out wherever a low-life can stay hidden with a big bankroll. She owed me three million. And I suspect she has more with her. Can you make a little time for ... this?

– A girl. A teenager. Owes you three million dollars. And you think she's carrying it with her. You're not serious.

He placed a small stack of 500 Euro notes on my desk.

– I'll explain later. I need more sleuthing and less questions right now. There wasn't any sort of ... personal relationship ... if you're getting any of those sorts of ideas.

I stared at it. Like I said, rent was overdue. And way back, deep down in the recesses of my mind where I try never to let sunlight or fresh air ... a thought of bigger money problems of my own and ... in any case it was a sweet gig as long as Dr. Weatherbottom or whatever today's fake name was understood where my work ended.

– Sure, I'm happy to take a crack at it for a couple of days. Let's be straight about this: I can try and find the girl. If I'm really lucky, I might get a little bit of evidence as to how much money she's working with here. But, at best, you get time and information. Worst case, you just get my time; I'm not making any guarantees. And under no circumstances am I trying to intervene with her to collect your money. That's on you.

– Understood. Let's start there. The payment is for forty-eight hours. I hope to get some information. If things go well, we can talk again after that.

Before I could say anything, he nodded, turned and nearly ran out of my office. I thought briefly about trying to catch him before he left the building; then I thought about tailing him. But I had enough to do. He was squirrelly as hell, but the job was small, legal, and lucrative.

And it interested me for another reason. I had seen the girl in the photo before, looking a little cleaner and a lot more scared. Only, when she talked to me, she called herself Lauren.

If Lauren were actually a street kid, I'd know right where to start looking. Small town and all that. But this was way more complicated. She had said something about a friend in southwest, but that's a huge area with no street grid: it's ridges, ravines, isolated neighborhoods. Even if you had police units prowling for her and a helicopter with infrared to help and coordinate, it would be a long shot. And even if I could sex up the story enough to interest the cops, PPB didn't have units to spare and could barely pay for the 100LL gas in its Cessna. A helicopter is still a dream out here. Oh, also: people lie.

She had a phone but as yet I hadn't received her promised text and, realistically, I didn't expect to, so I didn't have her number.

But, I thought, on the off chance she isn't swapping SIMs on the regular, Weatherson just might.

I thought about dialing him at the Nines. But then I had a better idea: I could stretch my legs with a fifteen minute walk and see if anyone I knew there was working today. Then maybe I could learn some more about the doctor—if he even was a doctor. I still planned to contact him but I wanted to get myself briefed and oriented going into that encounter.

And, in any case, it had been thirty-six hours since San Roman pressed me into service and I hadn't accomplished a thing for him. I did get shot at, which was a fairly decent excuse for the delay, but it wasn't on his case. Having a weirdo "doctor" show up with a stack of cash? That was less violent and also not on his case: it wouldn't buy any further time.

For the San Roman work, I had almost nothing: some video clips and stills and whatever the opposite of a head start is called.

I had to do something... Starting at "the pit" or at Blanchet House and hearing incoherent stories in exchange for a dozen pills' worth of cash just didn't appeal. The one advantage, if I could call it that, of the police having both interest and a jump on me in Ara's attack was the tiny chance a detective on the force would share. I texted my one guy in the role. Detective Brendan Whidby. "Witless" to his friends, and we were pretty close after eight days in a metaphorical foxhole getting compulsory fincrime training from the feds. Actually, it wasn't the days, but the drinking beer and sweating in a humid foul-smelling Virginia motel by night that forged the bond. He replied that he had a few minutes to meet.

Several filthy blocks later, I was at Kelly's Olympian and spotted Witless in the small place immediately. Over pints of Big Booty, I shared how I had been Shanghaied by Bain and taken the gig for San Roman.

– So that's what you've been spending your time on? And I heard you shot someone already on this case.

– No. I mean I did shoot someone. But that's another case entirely. One at a time would be too simple. With San Roman and Ara, I've got zero so far. Your guys have almost a day on me though, so I thought maybe...

– Yeah, I've got something, not much. Maybe you put your brain to work and make it make sense: this is a funnier one than it looked at first glance. Like, right off, San Roman isn't a hundred percent cooperative. He's pretending to be cooperative, gave us the videos, the angry rah-rah git-'em speech, details about Ara ... but something seemed just a touch off for both of the detectives that talked to him.

– You get any sense what was going on?

He took advantage of the interruption to swig some beer. Mine was already a third gone.

– Couldn't put a finger on it but it's just something you learn to smell. We start chasing it down—not a ton to go on with the pics—looking for people in the area, doing the fusion stuff with other cameras. Meanwhile, we hear through the grapevine how he's after Bain to bring you in and we haven't even been working it twelve hours?

He paused for more beer.

– But that's just nothing. Vibes. It gets better. We're collecting info from everybody who had interacted with Ara before the incident—staff at San Roman's place—and while I'm talking to that butler, there's a cook walks in and sees the video footage up on my laptop. She asks me to play it again. I ask her, "Why?" She says, "The guy walks a little funny." I'm telling you, we should hire this cook into the detective division.

She watches that video on loop for about a minute and says she's seen that guy before. Of course I don't know how rare the guy's walk is—we'll get a guess from the nerds soon—but given we don't have much of anything else and we're gonna be on the evening news, it could be huge. So where has she seen the guy? She's not sure. It was a while ago. But maybe on the way to work or at work, she says. And so you see where this is going: if it was at work—at San Roman's place—then maybe this guy had been visiting ... or prowling ... which opens up a few more paths to track him.

– The cook didn't have anything else?

– I don't think so. If she did, she wasn't giving it up.

– Because there's another possibility if he was at San Roman's. Like maybe he worked on something there? Or even worked for the family at some point, God knows they've got a payroll.

– A sort of inside job?

– Well that makes it sound more sinister than what I had in mind. But it's always a possibility. Not typical in an assault like this, but nothing about Ara and her family are remotely typical. In any case, I gotta tell San Roman when we meet tomorrow.

– Do what you gotta do but you better obscure the trail really goddamned well. There's press here from countries I've never even heard of. You know the drill.

– Yep. I'll juggle it, man. This is a tough one for me and I get that it's extra risky for you.

– You come talk to me when you decide to trade that plastic card for a badge. Or, well, for a different plastic card. The analysts don't get badges.

He laughed and quickly finished the beer. Mine was already gone.

– Ok, I'm outta here.

I clapped him on the back as he turned toward the door. A minute later, after checking my phone, I followed, ducking into yet another hotel, across the street, to call San Roman and mentally rehearse my play at the Nines. The lobby space here—maybe they gave it some branded name like "The Living Room" or "The Library" the way some places did—was a brilliantly designed, warm space. It theatrically evoked nineteenth- and early-twentieth-century fantasies of opulence without being realistic enough to expose hard edges, such as any spot away from the fire being frigid.

It was unclear how long the property could remain operating near fentanyl ground zero, but, in the meantime, any foot traffic—even mine—livened the place up. I kept trying to persuade a junior manager, Andrea, to put coffee in the lobby for guests, but I think she knew it would basically be my coffee and make the place way more attractive than my office. So, instead, she once again referred me to the pop-tune-filled modern coffee monstrosity at the end of the block. I declined. Sitting in a delightful red velvet chair, I picked up the phone uncaffeinated and dialed.

Ricardo didn't pick up and I opted to leave a minimal message assuring him of some valuable progress. I'd save the details for when I either knew more, was more desperate, or had to face his presence again. He wasn't a sucker though, and he knew I knew it. So I wrapped up the message asking if he'd ever hired anyone with a bow leg or a bit of a turned ankle.

I was improvising. A lack of medical training left me bereft of even the vocabulary for the gait issue. Just as well since all I had was the video. On to the mad doctor, as I had started calling him in my mind.

I walked the block and a half to the Nines to scope things out. The Nines operated in the Meier and Frank Building, a magnificent white landmark adjacent to the Pioneer Courthouse and diagonally across from the square. The building had been the flagship of the Meier and Frank department store chain and had maintained the legendary glamor of the urban department store era into the twenty-first century. Then retail evolution caught up with the business and the Nines set up shop in most of the building. The hotel kept it occupied and operating for over a decade before Covid and riots eviscerated the remaining office space and the retail at ground floor. The Nines made it through all that, though, in decent form, and put the massive central atrium to good use providing bar, restaurant, and lobby space plus people watching from guest rooms.

Luck was with me today: Michael Freeley, the property's restaurant and catering manager, was in and could be counted on for gratitude and assistance. For sixteen months, a sophisticated group had been exfiltrating guest credit card numbers—mostly from the restaurant's systems—and every time they thought they had the tech cleaned up, more cards would be compromised. Together, he and I had shut that operation down, a great collaboration of IT and human detection. So, if he could get away with it, he'd happily let me peek at Doc Weatherson's record in their system.

Indeed that plan worked out. But twenty minutes later the only things I had really learned were his credit card number (banks don't spill to people like me) and that he or his party really liked fresh Pacific oysters. Like about two hundred bucks' worth of oysters just that day.

I headed to a corner of the lounge, picked up a house phone, and asked the desk to connect me to the doc. He was happy to hear from me and seemed genuinely regretful he had not given me Lauren's number at my office. He claimed that since he had been pursuing her for the money, she had blocked him completely and so he had given up the number and forgotten about it. The story was plausible. I thanked him and told him I hoped she was still on that line because, if so, I could take a swing at a location. He thanked me in turn and seemed about to hang up when he paused and said: "If you make progress, keep things tight, don't let anyone else pick up the trail by watching you. Good luck." He hung up.

That, I thought, was a pretty incongruous close. The doc knew someone else was after Lauren but hadn't said anything? Clearly, a lot was left out of the story for my benefit ... which is a fairly common problem in my line of work. But, in this case, we already had shots fired and a scared young girl—albeit a shady one—supposedly on the run with millions of dollars on or near her person.

It was time to get some answers. A reverse house call was in order.

I headed to the elevator and was joined by two other men in PNW tourist wear. The doors closed.

As soon as the elevator started moving, I realized I had made a mistake. Working a high-rise hotel is tricky with a two-man team, almost impossible with one. After the last seventy-two hours, too much coffee, and a beer, I was starting to feel it. I should have planned this encounter better but I just couldn't let it go and in a stupid move—the kind that gets people killed—I jumped into the elevator without carefully checking the lobby. I didn't think anyone had made me.

As the car passed the tenth floor, I felt iron in my side. My arm slowly dropped toward my holster.

– Don't. You're not that stupid. And you suspect that I just might be.

He was right. I slowly got my hands where he could see them.

– When it stops, walk out in front of me and go right. Room 1323.

The elevator doors opened. My eyes darted around. There were no good options. One man peeled off and walked the hallway; the other handed me a key card and stayed behind me. Once inside the room, he took my gun, patted me down, looked through my wallet. I was sitting on the edge of the bed and he stood facing me, his back to the door. His full-size automatic, more than twice the size of mine, was in a relaxed grip next to his thigh.

– Ok, ok, "investigator," eh? Like, a fancy rent a cop?

– Actually, yeah, a lot like that. These days...

I was stalling, hoping he wasn't in a rush. He cut me off.

– Makes sense. Well, it doesn't totally make sense. But this explains a few things. You're sloppy. But we're both on the job here, so you spill it and we part ways in peace.

How much did he know? What could I get away with? I took a flier.

– We're trying to get a handle on the luxury boosting biz. There's a guy here who's two levels up in the org and we want to collect some more intel for a bust. Cops won't get involved until we've done ninety-nine percent of the work for them ourselves.

A shitty cover story, but not implausible.

– The fuck you are.

He didn't stop looking at me while he popped the mag on my .380 and fingered the rounds out into his palm, dumped them in his pocket, and tossed the empty mag on the floor. The gun was on the mattress. I had a spare ten-round mag hidden in my shoe. Not easy, but the gears started slowly turning.

– How about you fill me in clear and quick, I get out of here and you live to fight another day.

An old one but I thought to try it. I tilted my head like I was thinking.

– Know anything about Jim Berkmand?

With my left hand I started scratching at my neck ... while slowly pivoting my right foot back, heel upward, just eight inches or so from my other hand dangling next to the mattress.

– No idea what you're talking about. You got about five seconds if you want to be conscious when I walk out of this room.

– Ok, Berkmand was working for a chip factory in Hillsboro and passing corporate secrets when his bosses hired me.

The hidden mag was out of my shoe and in my hand.

– Anna Carlsson? Dr. Anna Carlsson?

If he had hesitated a half second longer before saying, "Big mistake," I'd have had him—at least in my own mind. The last thing that went through that mind was wondering who carries a metal-frame gun anymore. Then my skull exploded and I took a cruise through the starless sky of the underworld for ... well ... I guess about five hours.

It was better than a guess because when I started to reemerge into the prior universe, I still had my watch. I'd heard of cases where kidnappers mess with a captive's watch to distort their sense of time, but that was atypical. I had the word "atypical"—which felt like a sign my head wasn't as full of cotton balls nor as split wide open as it felt. Still, I could barely move, barely breathe, and felt like I was roasting ... but I wasn't tied up or tied to anything. Instead, I was in some sort of nylon wrapping. After struggling for a minute and noticing the exquisite fluff of my fabric prison, I realized I was zipped—completely—into a sleeping bag. I found the zipper, but it wouldn't give.

My pockets were empty. No knife or keys. My fingernails were way too smooth to tear the bag. This was deeply uncomfortable to say nothing of humiliating. Goddamnit.

Ok, the zipper slider wouldn't budge. The outer pull tab must be fastened. Now, just supposing my abductors weren't connoisseurs of quality camping and outdoor gear, the zipper might be vulnerable elsewhere.

The bag was so tight—a mummy job—that I had no hope of getting to the zipper stop. But a crappy zipper ... I pinched the plastic and nylon zipper where I could reach it, twisted it like I was wringing out a towel, trying to work a little too much space between the teeth as the whole thing flexed. Then if I could get a fingernail into the gap...

It took me twelve or thirteen tries over the course of what was probably six minutes, despite feeling like an hour. I had popped a couple of teeth out, and ripped a hole open.

Gratefully, I gulped in cool external air, but held as still as I could manage. For all I knew, the sleeping bag was in the middle of a room and watched over by a couple of hard guys.

It was dark outside the bag and the ground under me didn't feel like a floor. I saw no lights at first except the stars and heard a rushing sound. Peeking farther out and twisting my head revealed a lot of nothing. I made a little more noise. No sign of anyone emboldened me and I ripped the bag open the rest of the way. I emerged from my chrysalis to learn the camping was neither metaphor nor bad joke. I was in the woods. The rushing was a stream.

Without a better sense of my location, going anywhere could be deadly. But I didn't want to wait until sunrise.

I carefully probed the ground in a circle. There was a smooth section. Feeling that further revealed an edge on the other side. And a trail. With exquisite slowness, I worked my way ten, then twenty feet along the trail heading downslope. It was possible to move but I wouldn't cover any distance at this pace. I went another twenty feet. The trail paralleled the stream. Ok, just twenty more feet. Roughly halfway through, I saw lights—a few in the trees at a distance and some brighter ones down the trail below me. I could almost see the trail now. Another hundred fifty feet and I emerged at a small parking lot with a bench and bus shelter. The benches boasted metal stencils with the name "Linnton." I knew where this was. The bastards had tossed me in the woods off of Route 30, about ten miles north of downtown.

It was a few minutes before ten at night, so there wouldn't be a bus here until morning. But, if I hustled, I could walk across the towering gothic-styled St. Johns Bridge to the supermarket on the other side before it closed. That would be the nearest realistic access to the world I felt I'd left. I shook my head to clear it—something I immediately regretted because the pain flared up again violently—and took off at a brisk, if wobbly, walk.

I reported my own abduction to the Portland Police Bureau from the phone of a Safeway cashier. At first, it took a bit of persuading that I wasn't a bum, a lunatic, or both. Leaving out most of the salient details surrounding the events at the

Nines, stretching the credulity of the dispatcher at the distant North Precinct, and refusing EMS transport finally got me a ride home and brief interview with a cop I had met a couple of times while working. I think he appreciated the entertaining sleeping bag elements of the story and didn't press me too much on the Nines bit, although he said if anyone takes a closer look ... well. Yeah, I get it.

I stumbled up to bed.

10

I woke up to my phone buzzing on the nightstand and about a dozen voicemails from Sgt. Berkson, from San Roman, from ex-commissioner Bain, and from "Dr. Weatherson"—not necessarily in that order.

It was only 9 a.m.

Complete chaos had opted for an early start. Nothing made any sense at all. From what I could reconstruct via the voicemails and texts, around 7:30 a.m., Ara had been walking near the hospital and things had gone crazytown from there.

I wasn't even awake and the questions started multiplying.

Ara was up and about? Was she discharged? Did they just let her go out for a walk?

And she was talking at a bus stop by the hospital with the girl I knew as Lauren. What was the connection there?

And then the kicker: our friends in the Charger drove by and tried to shoot Lauren full of holes—but put the lead in Ara instead. Lauren apparently disappeared. Again. Ara survived and was back in the hospital in critical condition.

How did Weatherson know about any of this?

His message just told me to suspend the job and stay off Lauren's trail for twelve hours or until I heard from him again.

This time he called her Lauren... What the actual...? Why'd he make the switch? Did he not know the "Lauren" name before?

My head was spinning. I needed coffee. A lot of coffee. And a handful of Aleve, as many Tylenol as my liver could withstand, and a shot of vodka.

I had better start with just the coffee. I brewed the java wicked strong and poured a big cup, carried it downstairs, and suddenly felt weak. Like, low blood pressure, passing out weak. Sitting on a cracked concrete step with my back against the building holding my coffee, I was probably looking not entirely different from the four junkies out cold along the opposite side of the block.

That's not true. I was somewhat alert, which earned me requests for cigarettes and cash from two other junkies, one pulling a wagon and the other a baby carriage, both piled with bottles and blankets.

I smelled smoke but it wasn't weed, tobacco, or even fentanyl. There was a small bonfire warming a couple of guys diagonally across on the sidewalk. I dragged myself back up the stairs to wash up.

I felt a wreck. The booze was tempting and my brother had sent me an unusual bottle of Polish rye vodka that opened like biting into a giant peppercorn and closed with lime and it was in the freezer ice cold. Maybe I didn't deserve poetry like that. I was staring down the barrel of too much day for a morning shot. I took another cup of black coffee into the shower with me instead.

What were my options here? I had to return the calls and, at the very least, keep Bain and San Roman at bay for a bit … and Weatherson had another thing coming in my mind—even if (and I doubted it) he was ignorant of the free camping trip up north I had earned three doors down from his hotel room.

Talking to Berkson, on the other hand, held appeal, so I tapped his name and the phone dialed.

When I hung up, four minutes and forty-nine seconds later per the phone's screen, I didn't feel any better but I had learned a few additional facts. The drive-by appeared to be conducted from the same Dodge Charger I had encountered two days prior: visual and plates matched the video I took in Old Town. This recent attempt also seemed a touch more serious. The shooter stayed in the car and dumped thirty-three rounds during a slow roll, fully auto. Ara, Lauren, two techs, and a doc were also waiting for the bus and it was a minor miracle no one was killed and only Ara got hit.

How did the cops know the shooters were after Lauren and not Ara? They didn't know but took a working assumption from the purple Charger and the shooter making eye contact with Lauren (and only her) before opening fire. Repeat: working assumption.

I then made two quick, defensive-play calls to Bain and to San Roman to rent some time.

I had decided my best next move was to spend that time hunting down Weatherson and politely insisting on the rest of his story.

11

I didn't even have Weatherson's phone number. That was step one.

Trying easy mode first, I dialed the Nines, had them call Weatherson and give him a message, get him to call me.

Wait five minutes. He called in two. I didn't answer but I had his number now.

Next, the harder step: either tracking his phone or finding out where it was.

The cops could track his number, at least approximately. But I didn't think I'd get any help on this angle from them, at least not soon. Of course I had access to some sketchy online services that sometimes produced recent geolocations, and I could even try and drop spyware on his phone if it really came to that.

But there was no need to start with hard and approximate techniques. With this much caffeine in me, I was ready to roll old school with some social engineering. I called the Nines again, asked for his room. I didn't get an answer, which added weight to my guess that he was not there.

Now for the fun part: from a blocked number, I called his phone and, this time, with a rough alteration of my voice, I *was* the Nines. Housekeeping had come across something sensitive in his room—extremely sensitive—and as a courtesy we wanted him to consider taking possession of it if it was his ... otherwise we would need to call the police immediately. We couldn't discuss it by phone, but already had sent a car to pick him up, if he could just let us know where to direct the driver.

He was clearly agitated and confused but revealed he was at the downtown Hilton where he said he had met a colleague for coffee. I assured him he wouldn't have long to wait and we'd call him back. The first part was indeed true if the second wasn't.

I hopped the MAX to the Hilton. It was time for a few answers.

12

Eight minutes later, I followed a guest entering the Hilton from Broadway, figuring twenty-to-one Weatherson would be a floor down on the opposite side, expecting the car at the main entrance.

I skulked around the edge of the lobby until I spotted him standing just inside the main doors.

I came up alongside him and clapped him around the shoulders.

– Howdy, doc!

I couldn't risk any wrestling right here, but, with this friendly gesture, if he tried to bolt, I'd get enough advance warning to subtly restrain him for a second or two and try to talk him out of it.

As it happened, he melted, terrified. Presumably not of me. He wasn't unhappy to see me and when I suggested we take a coffee to a corner in the mezzanine and chat, he was more than willing.

– Look, I'm glad you found me here. Not sure how it happened but I needed to talk to you. But I can't talk right now. There's a problem at my hotel. I don't know exactly what, but I have to –

I cut him off.

– There's no problem at the Nines. That was me. I'm sorry, doc, but there have been some ... developments ... in your case and I needed to get hold of you right away.

– Jesus Christ, man! What kind of spy-versus-spy bullshit is this? Why didn't you just ask?

– Well, first, I didn't have your phone number.

– Sorry, my ... that wasn't intentional.

– And honestly? Given the circumstances, I couldn't trust you to show up or stay put. I need to know a few things.

He relaxed. Not one hundred percent, but substantially. And a bit of the old surgeons' assertiveness came back into his voice.

– As much as I appreciate your help, I am hiring you, and so I expect to be able to keep my private –

Again, I cut him off.

– This is bigger than your case at the moment. There's murder—well, at the very least, attempted murder—and some high profile people involved. Maybe not by Seattle standards, but enough to make sure the authorities here will take a really close look at you...

I paused for dramatic effect.

– Unless...

Another pause.

– Unless you can help me fill in some blanks and find some more plausible villains for the story. And just look—I picked up a paper featuring Ara on the front page off a stack of *Ore-*

gonians on a nearby coffee table and almost shook the paper at him—it is definitely a story.

He wasn't a tough guy and he wasn't pretending to be. His eyes darted around like a trapped animal. In a near whisper he asked if we could go somewhere more private. I asked what he had in mind and he said his hotel room.

I thought about my last visit—or attempted visit—and weighed the risk against the increased comfort and, hopefully, increased candor his room might induce over the spartan environment of my office. More than one client had compared the experience of visiting my office to visiting his divorce lawyer but with cheaper decor. It amplified the sense of discomfort which, to my mind, has its uses. Today, though, we needed a softer touch, so we went back to the Nines and despite my revulsion to the stuff I bought us a couple of a bourbons on eight to take upstairs.

13

Sitting on his bed, Weatherson swigged about half the glass before setting it on the nightstand and starting his story in a monotone.

– I'm just another loser who fucked up in Vegas, it's really as simple as that. I've got a bit of an ego and I fell for a classic. I thought I could play poker; I won some pots; I met some people; I got invited to bigger games. I might have been drugged, I'm not sure, but I shouldn't have drunk anything at all. I shouldn't have ever sat down at those tables. Most of the time I thought I was killing it so I didn't trust the losses. They played me up and down for thirty-five hours. All within a weekend. And I went home down about $800,000.

– Now, I've done well professionally. I have the house in Broadmoor, the boat, the club membership. As for the wife, well, I wouldn't say she takes it for granted, but her life is built around her friends there. The kids in school: son at Stanford, daughter at Pepperdine Law. I'm nearly the best transplant surgeon in Seattle and I have it good. But I still work for a living, in a manner of speaking. U-Dub is a public school. I make a bit on the side but I don't have a spare million sitting around to settle a debt. Things got really dark. And then this girl shows up and offers me a way out.

– She didn't know about my situation. Well, fuck, I mean it didn't even occur to me to think she did. Maybe someone tipped her off. She said she was just trying to save her brother. Black sheep of the family. Dad had plenty of money and the medical connections but the two kept fighting. For years. And now the boy needed a kidney fast or he was going to die. The girl had the money. Crypto. She said she was a courier for a drug importer—never touched the drugs, just carried the hardware with passphrases for the wallets, usually three, four million dollars at a time, between Portland and Vancouver, BC. She told me how she got involved. She might have been full of shit but she seemed quite proud of herself. Rich girl rebel and all that. One day she took the latest passphrase, transferred everything to a new wallet, and, instead of flying to BC, she came to my office.

– "Jessica" she called herself, by the way. Jessica so-called put about $80,000 in gold on my desk. Like actual metal gold. Said to think about getting a clean kidney into her brother and she'd be back tomorrow. I know this all sounds crazy but you gotta understand where I was at: I had already started secretly borrowing to make a payment on the Vegas losses. They said they'd accept some payments while I worked out the rest but, without those installments, they'd visit me at home right away. I took the gold to get it looked at in a pawn shop downtown. With a spectrometer. And it checked out.

– The next day, the girl shows up with another pile of gold. Said she wanted to do it in crypto but wasn't sure I was young enough to understand that the locked metal card she had stashed in town was really the keys to about four million dollars. Kids. My own are like that too. But I get how crypto works. I went to one of those investor seminars. So she let me poke around her wallets myself while she watched. The coins were there.

– I said I'd need at least a day to think about it. But less than eight hours later I was on the phone telling her I'd just need a little time to line up suppliers, a facility, assistants and in the meantime she could bring her brother to my private clinic for a quick exam.

– The whole thing was like a bad dream. But I played it out. The boy had a new kidney in him within a week and I didn't even know his name. I had a half million from her at that point, but that just covered my, um, costs. I was supposed to get two million more.

I put on my most sympathetic face.

– Lemme guess. Then they disappeared?

– Not right away. It was almost worse what happened. They knew the transplant was risky, they just wanted to make sure there were no immediate complications and that I wouldn't say anything to anyone. Heck, I had way more to lose than they did—I was gonna take this whole thing to my grave. But the kid is freaked out and she doesn't understand all that. She sent me $50,000 each day for a week and a half. I was waiting to do a follow up exam in my clinic. And they came in, but he was injured. Seriously injured. Gunshots and also a beating with some kind of blunt object. I was pretty sure he wasn't going to make it and there was nothing I could do. I told her to drive him to the trauma center—Harborview—right the hell now. It was his only chance, I told her. I checked later and a pair fitting their description made it to Harborview. The miracle workers managed to stabilize the boy. They left the hospital in rough shape two days later.

– Then I didn't hear from her. After three days I called her up. She wouldn't tell me anything. Just said we were done. I tried a few more times and she blocked me on her phone. From her money-running gig and little scraps she and her brother had let slip, I was pretty sure she would be here in Portland sooner or later. I think they're both from here originally. I inquired with some friends and friends of friends and that's how I ended up outside your office. And now I, I...

He seemed on the verge of tears, but he didn't cry or say much else. Drank the last of his whiskey and just looked at me.

I gestured at his glass; he nodded. I trusted him to stay put for five minutes so I went down to the bar and brought him up another drink.

– And where does she fit into all this? I asked, gently unfolding the newspaper with Ara's picture onto the bed.

– No fucking idea. No fucking idea.

A long pause, then he spoke up.

– Just tell me what to do.

For now – I explained – the best thing would be to hole up where no one could find him.

– We have two things to worry about: first, at some point your family or your colleagues are going to wonder where you are, right? Come up with a story for them, buy yourself at least a few days. Don't mention where you are. Then there's the local angle. What you're telling me explains why thugs are chasing Jessica, er, Lauren, or whoever she really is. They want the cartel crypto back or they need to kill her. Maybe both, just to send a message to the next courier with an entrepreneurial streak.

He protested. He wasn't really mixed up in that part of things. He had never got his hands on the real chunk of cash he was after. He'd just forget the whole thing and go home and they'd leave him alone. I thought to myself: this sounds a bit like the "bargaining phase" but I kept that to myself and just spoke in a calm, slow, and sober voice.

– You're mixed up in the middle of this now. These particular guys aren't white collar crooks, accountants or lawyers or anyone you're used to. They're gunmen. If they don't succeed, the higher ups will just send better, more experienced gunmen. Your job is to stay one hundred percent out of sight until the cops find Lauren, I find her ... or ... the gangsters find her. We can hope that will bring the matter to an end in some way. But until then...

– Yes, I get it. I'll figure out something with work and the wife. And this hotel is no good?

– Afraid not. Somebody grabbed me here the first time I came to talk to you. Long story. I don't know exactly who but it was not likely a coincidence. Let's do this. I'll have a bag brought up to your room in about an hour. Old clothes, a few other things. Get yourself up like a bum. Make sure you can wrap a blanket over your head and really fit in with the sketchiest people around here. I'll wait for you at the loading dock, you come out and I'll walk you to a different hotel. One where I have a bit more pull with the security team and you'll either be safe or—worst case—we'll get a solid heads up before anyone gets to you.

14

And that's exactly how it went. It's embarrassing how many times I've done the same thing and I suppose it will keep working until the normies come back to downtown. Then I'll need to dress my clients and witnesses in sportswear. In the meantime: Grab some laundry bags. Raid the lost and found. Spill a bunch of coffee, ketchup, and mayo and then rip the clothes a bit. Hit the pharmacy on the corner at Broadway to get anything else we might need.

Downtown Portland has short blocks and no alleys, which makes it harder to skulk, sneak, and surveil here than in other places. For example, the Nines' loading dock and "back entrance" is right onto the sidewalk at the middle of Alder, the next block. Since Covid, though, that hasn't been much of a problem; most days, Portland's downtown streets are emptier than a Chicago alley at midnight.

Half an hour later, doc stumbled out the back of the hotel half wrapped in that thin nasty blanket you only see on the beds of really cheap hotels or, occasionally, in the foldout bed kit at a nicer one.

He followed me staying half a block back and we both got to the Multnomah after a few minutes. I kept doc "under wraps" until I got ahold of Manny Gil. We sat in the security office and I shared the lay of the land ... or at least as much of it as Manny needed to know.

He was helpful as ever. The hotel was full because of the conference. But there were a number of rooms with busted climate control which couldn't be rented and doc was welcome to one of those. No maid service, of course, which suited us fine. Manny even offered me an adjoining room if I wanted to keep tabs on the doc, which I at first declined and then, after a moment's thought, accepted. It wasn't a bad idea, at least for tonight.

We put doc to bed with strict instructions not to use the room phone nor to open up for anything or anyone. I promised him food from the restaurant downstairs, let him keep his phone but gave him that "friendly uncle" look again and said anytime he's tempted to do something silly with his phone, remember what you're about to see. Manny looked on as I showed him a bit of footage. It was the video I had shot after my first encounter with the violent enforcers chasing Lauren's stolen loot.

Manny momentarily tensed up at the footage then relaxed. The doc didn't notice and seemed suitably impressed with the gangsters. So I left him watching TV, muted with the captions on, and took the elevator down with Gil.

– When did you take that video? And where? Might have a lead for you if you can tell me.

– A few days ago down the street. By my office. First time I had to shoot in a while. Seemed out of the blue, but I'm starting to put some pieces together.

– Well here's another piece for you: remember the weird snatch-and-grab, with the laptop case, where you got beaned?

He gestured toward my head.

It felt like a year ago but, still, how could I forget? When I touched the relevant spot on my skull, it lit up with fireworks. I winced.

– What about it?

– The guys came back a couple of times. We ran them off. But we got a better look each time and I'm eighty percent certain one of them is the guy in your video. What's all this about?

I thought about how far to go here. Manny and I went back a long way so I figured the hell with it.

– If it's the same crew, then they're enforcers looking for a few million in stolen drug money and the girl that took it.

– And some of the cash was in the laptop case? Or they thought it was?

– In a manner of speaking. These guys are using crypto wallets now, and the only thing that has to physically move is a secure container for keys: a thin little metal gadget. That was probably what they were after in the laptop case. If the girl they're after was—or had been—here, that could be a lucky break. For the enforcers then, but for us now. But it seems unlikely. I wonder what sent those guys here...

– Well, I can look. I have some time on my hands this afternoon. Got a picture of the girl?

I showed him a pic then sent it to him.

– Let me know if you find anything. I'm going to grab some food for me and our guest, and head upstairs for the night.

I did that, checked the hall doors, left the communicating door open a foot or so.

What next?

Topping the list was probably bringing Lauren "in from the cold" while she was still warm, if there was any chance of that. She was probably holed up good for the night ... I hoped ... and finding her would have to wait for tomorrow. I flipped over and fell dead asleep.

15

I dreamed of chases through endless hotel corridors. Doors opened into service hallways for conference and banquet halls. My own personal backrooms. And I awoke to the sound of breaking glass. I popped up, looked around. Light leaked into the room through the gap in the draperies. Nothing moved.

I crawled out of bed and prowled toward the communicating door. Still nothing. Got to Weatherson's bed and he was fast asleep. The glass breaking must have been in another room or in the hallway.

I wrote the doc a note on the hotel stationery to avoid waking him with any sort of ringtone, went down to eight and collected some breakfast to go, deposited it in the room along with another note (admonishing the doctor not to leave the room under any circumstances), and wandered out into a cool, gray, and drippy Portland morning.

Pacing around Pioneer Courthouse Square, I tried the simplest approach to finding Lauren: dialing the number Weatherson had shared. *Mirabile dictu*—especially given her age—she answered. Then again, winding up on the wrong end of a few dozen 9mm rounds has a curious power to change old habits and create receptivity to new ones ... at least the first few times it occurs.

I took a deep breath as she wore herself out spewing a stream of invective at me, thematically oriented around my failure to protect her from the prior morning's attack. When the swearing gradually gave way to crying, I gently reminded her that I had no idea where she was, she hadn't contacted me, and by the way I had been kidnapped among other things while tracking down her info. Which was mostly true and was, in any case, persuasive. She cut the tears so easily they seemed suspect then told me she had an idea who might be after her, followed by a smooth transition into asking if I could lend her a gun.

As if there was any chance that would happen.

– I've got a couple of leads on the guys as well, I told her.

A partial truth.

– And?

– I think they're down from Vancouver. Drug cartel enforcers. They're sloppy because they're the low-level disposable help. Probably why you're still alive.

– Why are they after me? Can't the police arrest them ... or the DEA or somebody?

Now was the time to make my move.

– I think I'm close to putting together more info on them, maybe enough to get them off your back for good with the help of the PPB, but I need to talk to you in person first.

– Why?

She sounded suspicious.

– I, uh, know you might not be one hundred percent squeaky clean in all this –

She interrupted with a "You motherfucker!" followed by another twenty-odd seconds of swearing.

I let it run a bit and then cut back in.

– Look, none of that matters if you're dead and I think I can prevent that. But you need to work with me. Where can I find you?

Silence for about ten seconds. Then she spoke up.

– Go down the Springwater along the river about a mile. Around to where the Oaks Bottom parking lot is. But all the way down by the water, below the path. I'll be there with a friend at 6 p.m. tonight. Look for the blue and gray tent. There's a bunch of other folks hanging out there too so keep it cool.

It actually wasn't the craziest place to hide out, at least for the short term.

– Ok. I'll meet you. You need anything there?

My avuncular side was poking its head.

– No, I... Wait, actually, yeah. Can you bring five hundred in cash? I'm good for it, I swear.

If the doc's story was even remotely true, then that was an understatement.

– What for the five hundred?

– There's a guy here with a boat. It's pretty messed up but it'll float in the lagoon.

– Not a bad plan. I'll bring it.

I lied. I mean, it was a sensible plan the way she was looking at the world, but it wouldn't work for more than a few days. Unless she ditched the phone, really went dark, and survived the junkies on the river somehow ... the pros would get to her and it would end badly (if she gave up the crypto wallet immediately) or much worse (if she tried not to).

– Thanks.

She disconnected. I sat down in the brickwork amphitheater of the square and checked my mail.

There was an email from Sgt. Berkson with a big file attachment. "Security footage from the bus stop at OHSU. Good luck."

A big monitor and a decent laptop would be needed to take a close look so I headed to the office.

Entry was uneventful—as it nearly always was—but I was half expecting to be accosted by a new visitor at the outside entrance or, given the shaky security situation, inside.

A second email had joined the first during the walk across Burnside.

Now I had two sets of videos, both featuring our troubled teen turned thief.

In the first videos, from OHSU, Lauren was visible walking up to Ara, who was standing and pacing, maybe vaping, playing with her phone. They talk for about a minute, body language tense or even aggressive, before the Charger comes driving across the corner of the frame, Lauren takes off running past Ara, and disappears out a different corner of the frame while Ara gets thrown against a wall and then collapses under the influence of lead.

There was something immediately off about the video. Not "wrong" off per se, like it was AI generated or otherwise faked. Just ... something stuck in my mind watching it. Something that shouldn't be there ... besides, of course, a hospital bus stop taking thirty-plus rounds of 9mm.

I watched it a couple of additional times but couldn't quite pin down the issue so I turned to the next email and its videos.

That second email was from Manny Gil and it featured Lauren entering the lobby via the south entrance and working her way into and out of several conference rooms before exiting the hotel to the west. Manny had recognized Lauren from the photo fairly quickly after I left. She had gotten herself into a little trouble in the lobby cafe, which was the only reason he had pulled clips of her off the security network video recorder.

The clips didn't connect—lots of isolated cameras—but the timestamps lined up. Apparently the security system "knew" all the clips were Lauren via some sort of clothing-based fingerprinting.

It was unclear why Lauren was ever in the Multnomah at all, but it could hardly be a coincidence.

I watched these latter clips a few more times, concluded that they amounted to little beyond evidence of Lauren's presence during the course of one hour, and went back to the earlier video. I let it play on loop about ten times before I needed to clear my head.

There were bits and pieces here, some critical information, and maybe even some answers. But the things I knew tangled up my head and ran me in circles. And there was a part I couldn't even articulate yet, like whatever nagged me in the bus stop drive-by video.

No amount of inner monologue could help me at this point. I had that feeling, where the next step would have to come by way of trees. I had about six hours before I had to set up for the meeting with Lauren.

16

Volcanic eruptions over sixteen million years ago created the Tualatin Mountains—more colloquially known as the west hills—separating Portland from the farms and burbs of Washington County. The Chinook lived there for ten thousand years before Portlanders logged some trees and later decided to save the rest. A massive, temperate rainforest that dwarfs all of the city's industrial and high-density development combined, Forest Park makes downtown Portland look like an island city in an ocean of trees: a mimeograph reverse of New York's Central Park open space. Frederick Law Olmsted connects them both and I had often wondered if this mirror-image pattern on east and west coasts of the continent ever flickered in his mind.

I needed to get my mind above all of it—metaphorically and physically. I needed altitude, abstraction, and a longer sweep of time. So I took the streetcar to the Slabtown garage where I kept a 2015 Mustang. Of course the one with the 435 horsepower V8 and of course in "triple yellow." It was the last toy I bought with what I had begun to call my dirty insurance money ... although in retrospect it's not clear the money has gotten much cleaner.

This parking space was as safe as they come in downtown, which isn't saying much. Luckily, the junkies have no idea what anything is worth, so the worst that ever happened was a broken window and a stolen empty solid state drive that I kept in the glove box for offloading photos.

Today she looked as shiny as I had left her, and, not wanting to attract attention, I waited until I had driven a few blocks before letting out the engine. I headed up toward Skyline Boulevard and cranked it heading north. I stopped a few minutes before the Grange Hall, threw the car into a gravel pad off the side of the road and dove into the forest on foot with an unnatural thirst.

The wetness and chaotic growth of the woods forced my thoughts away from simplistic logic and tactics. Here, things went sideways every moment of every day. The basic chemistry was predictable. But the weather driving the chemistry was not. The biology made out of the chemistry added a new layer of chaos. Yet, stepping back and looking at the trees, flowers, and ferns, listening to the birdsong, some aggregate predictability and order once again emerged.

The Douglas fir rules the years until one moment when that diseased weak spot, that eroded soil from last year's rains, that strong gust randomly catching one more branch becomes just too much ... and then 80,000 pounds of timber comes crashing down sideways, rerouting the very brook which had undermined it, indifferently crushing a nest of birds while sparing a warren of rabbits.

Things build and grow until they can't and then suddenly there is change. It seems simple, but we never know where the limit is or how big the collapse will be. We cannot know. It's a paradox: we can have all the causes yet never in enough detail—they combine and multiply from molecules to murderers until the land slides. That earth violently moves but we're stuck using clumsy gloves to handle soft aggregates: averages and temperatures, a theorem that tells us we're all going to die but we can't know when.

It can feel like watching a boiling pot, trying to pick the next tiny bubble to break loose from the bottom. We draw, we fire, we're often close but almost always too late. Sure, we hit sometimes, but, even then, things often don't turn out as desired.

The rainforest, trails decomposing under your feet as you walk them, trees crumbling into wet mulch and soaking your pants as you sit on them even in summer—they are not merely a distraction from a figurative concrete jungle. They speak about viruses, bank robbers, and the movement of tectonic plates—it's all the same lesson. The lecture bubbles and whirs, cracks and sings in the trees subtle but thundering, and if I stay long enough it penetrates down through the clever linguistic metaphors in my crusty frontal cortex until some deeper parts of my brain start responding and throbbing in rhythm.

Problem solving has a flavor, a feeling, a tickle deep in the brainstem. A sense or a smell that I can't quite place or grasp. But it leads me on where before there was no track. It's a wisp, a scent on the wind, I can almost place it. I walk where it leads, sometimes losing it entirely, hoping to catch just a bit ... a bit of something, can't place it, a faint color. Lilacs at dusk? But how? Why?

It's not that. It's gone. It's there but different. It's not lilac. It's lily white; it only looks purplish with the sun low in the sky. But why do I smell it? What am I doing? And now it's not even lily, it's the blades of grass under my bare feet as I wander the edges of the garden ... and then ... it's not the grass—it's the gaps in between tufts of grass, little empty moist flat spots and I stop and I remember thinking about how there's something I forgot to do, but it's deja vu, it's not real: I always think I was thinking that thought and I know it couldn't have happened. It's a repetitive undulating flow that sometimes goes nowhere.

Of course, once the empire falls and once the fawn chokes and dies in the burning of the wildfire, it had to have been that way. There was no other possible outcome. Essence of classical tragedy. All the more so because there was no way, even one moment before the inevitable, to know it for sure. The gods have truly cursed us with a foresight so persuasive and so brutally limited and we spend our lives trying to make everything different.

Look around. The Tualatin Mountains are millions of years old and not a single bug or branch has ever escaped. Everything breaks down, goes until it no longer does. This universe seems to have no sense of moderation while balance is visible only from a distance. The only stable patterns come from finding the right abstraction, the right level of granularity.

The rainforest became a rainforest once the first animal—maybe man, maybe not—thought of it as a thing. But even then it's an illusion: after all, we don't stroll icy wastes, parched deserts, or dead lava flows on Mars.

This all probably sounds pretty unhinged, but it's a helpful way to revise experience and discover what we don't think we know.

Humans, like trees or squirrels, are at once unpredictable and utterly predictable. Solving a crime means finding the aggregation of causes that made some outcome inevitable. The trick is that all these causes speak clearly only while in motion, in the past. After the fact they fall silent. Somewhere in between before and after is a pattern, that sweet spot of abstraction. Between unlikely cartoon simplicity and conspiracy theory tangle. Turning the focus on a microscope until the proper layer in the specimen comes crystal clear.

The key to crime—and to complexity—is in the interactions. Isolated elements don't do interesting things. But just one signal in the right place and...

I had it. Maybe. At least I had an idea which needed confirmation. About Lauren. She's fast like most teenage kids but she doesn't run quite right.

I was deep in the canyons now and it would take over an hour to get back to my Mustang. I felt good as I hoofed it up the hill.

17

I stomped the car onto Skyline and spun it around, a maneuver that was only remotely possible thanks to electronic traction and stability control. Kind of a cheat mode, but then again without it there's pretty much zero chance of driving four hundred horses around an Oregon winter.

Before my meeting with Lauren, I had just enough time to garage the car, clean up and swap some gear around, then make a phone call to check my new-found insight on that video.

Planning this call, I reflexively glanced down at my phone and saw it was blowing up. I swung the car off into a gravel pullout and stood on the brakes, again relying on the magic of microchips to make an impossible stop still facing the same direction.

There were a bunch of texts and messages but I got the gist instantly. Ara was dead.

18

I felt impatient about my hunch and felt an uncomfortable, anxious need to do something. So I stepped outside the car and called Sonia Parloff, a nurse at a regional hospital system whom I had dated for a brief spell. Things had ended on good terms and she still helped me track down medical info for work now and again. In this instance, I sent her the video clip from the drive-by as well as the clip from the original attack on Ara. She had no idea at first glance about the mildly odd walking and running—and I didn't expect her to—but she did say she could chat up an orthopedist and get back to me. I thanked her and promised—again—to make good on an overdue glass of wine. She laughed and reminded me that that hadn't worked well the last time and she'd happily take an ice cream or coffee in lieu during a break in an upcoming double shift. I promised that too.

I put the car away, took a streetcar and shoe leather—or rubber anyway—to my apartment, and got under a hot shower. With a towel wrapped around me I grabbed a stale week-old half Reuben sandwich from the fridge and wolfed it down, followed by some cold coffee. It was good enough for the purpose.

Lauren was a wild card in the extreme and so, getting dressed in dark gray, I planned for a potentially long, cold night down by the river. I grabbed the dirtiest backpack I owned and inserted a thick sweater and a rainproof outer shell. A flashlight, a small toolkit, first aid supplies, and extra magazines just about finished the packing list. As it would turn out, I was both radically over- and under- prepared. But the gear made sense in the moment.

I took a few minutes to sit back and strategize the meet, checked my phone, and found a message back already from Sonia. The ortho doc said he couldn't be sure without a proper exam or imaging, of course, but the unusual gait in the videos could stem from an uncommon congenital hip disorder. So, unless a lot of coincidence was at work, Ara's attacker and Lauren might well be related.

I considered how I might find a person using this new information. It seemed theoretically easy in that there would be few patients in the Portland area known to have that disorder and it would be in their insurance files and electronic medical records. But many cases might be undetected. And, even for the known cases, unless the patients had volunteered their info for some public cause, good luck searching the datasets or getting any of their names from a provider without a specific warrant.

So I didn't have a clear next step with the medical info, but it was definitely good enough for a solid report to San Roman. Heck, I thought, with his money and prior investments in a certain local health insurance player, he might even be able to turn up those names and help solve his own case. But with Ara killed just today, I wasn't looking forward to the conversation. If Lauren's and Ara's stories were connected—and it increasingly appeared they were—San Roman might very well assign me some of the blame for Ara. Grief drives people to all manner of madness and I didn't have a thick enough skin myself where innocent death was concerned to stay cool and try to wrangle him. I decided to wait on San Roman until tomorrow. It was a questionable call, but I told myself it was ok because I'd get more useful info out of Lauren once I had made some progress on her safety tonight.

19

I got the bus at the Burnside Bridge under the White Stag sign and rode it to the Oaks Bottom Refuge parking lot, near where Milwaukie crosses over Highway 99E. I walked down a quarter mile, took the side trail toward the river under the train tracks and then backtracked a quarter mile north on the Springwater bike path until my phone showed me in roughly the right place.

It was 5:30 p.m. and already getting dark under the Portland gray.

I stepped off the bike path, pulled on a beanie, and climbed down the slope into the woods. I worked my way around a mattress and a small mountain of partial bicycle carcasses. A gap in beaten-down bushes led to a grill and a generator that both looked like they might still work and then to a pile of empty jerry cans dripping their last gasoline into a rivulet of rainwater. The rivulet ran toward the Willamette.

Following the water led to a clearer trail and I followed that about two hundred feet toward the river. I slowed as I saw the first tents.

Making my way forward, one blue and gray tent appeared along with a green tent and some makeshift structures. I intentionally made some noise as I approached—I didn't want any-one to be surprised and react in a way that would add extra volatility to the situation. It worked: before I got within ten yards of the tent, a man emerged from behind a royal blue tarp anchored on a tree. He was another ten yards down river from where I stood.

I couldn't see his eyes but his overall demeanor was agitated and slightly spastic. He carried a partly rebuilt (or partly stripped—glass half empty I suppose) bicycle in one hand, al-most swinging it, as he came around the front of the tarp and stepped toward me.

– This isn't... This isn't a good place for you. You look like you probably shouldn't be here.

It was a little bit threatening but not over the top. I went for diplomacy.

– Yeah, I'm just trying to meet a friend. A girl. Hey, you need a cigarette?

– A girl. No, man. We don't do that kind of shit here. I know what you're talking about, but none of that here. We got enough trouble.

He looked down before continuing.

– If you really want a girl... Aw, man, no, probably it's not worth it. I'm not even gonna talk about where to go.

– No, not like that. Really, a girl I already know. I just need to talk to her. She told me to come here.

I held out two cigarettes in my left hand and pulled up a lighter in my right, took one more step, and stood still. The man kept swinging the bike frame, but slower. Ten seconds went by. Fifteen. He dropped the bike, came toward me, and reached for the smokes. He pocketed one and placed the other between his lips, took the lighter from my outstretched arm, lit up, and slowly handed back the lighter.

– Thanks.

I waited again as he took a couple of slow drags.

– I don't know about any girls around our place here. But Jimmy might.

He pointed upriver and walked along the bank to the blue and gray tent. I heard some low voices. He made his way back to me.

– Jimmy says there's a girl who gave him some stuff and said she'd be back around now but she isn't here. You want, you can wait a bit.

He gestured for me to follow and led me to an open area among the brush halfway to the tent. There was a tiny muddy hollow at water's edge where wood scraps were formed into a makeshift bench.

– I think she'll be coming from over there.

He pointed across the channel toward Hardtack Island.

I looked at him, confused. He gestured again and silently walked back toward his tarp. I sat on a broken four-by-four post at the edge of the water. Dusk was thickening and I couldn't see the details in the trees on the opposite bank, but I was looking.

After about five minutes, I got a sense that something was coming slowly across the water. The channel's about a hundred yards across here and soon I could tell there was a figure in a tiny boat at the halfway point. It slowly got closer and I could hear splashing—an irregular thrashing paddling. A minute later, I heard soft grunts and I realized the boat was an impossibly tiny and irregularly shaped dinghy. It listed and rocked as the figure struggled with a single paddle.

When it came within five yards, through the twilight haze, I recognized Lauren despite a hoodie. And what she was paddling wasn't even a boat. It was a scrap—it had been part of a boat once and now it had one or two other bits attached with marine epoxy. It was also sinking ... but that's not why it appeared to list: it was simply asymmetric to start with.

Lauren kept reaching for the bottom with one long paddle, finally caught it and almost lost her grip as it dug into the mud.

– Lauren! – I called out in a half whisper.

I wondered what state she would be in: she'd had heck of a time these past few weeks. And, like a lot of older teenagers, she had shown she could appear by turns mature and assertive, then naive and afraid. At seventeen, it wasn't usually an act. The rowdiest toughs were babies underneath, which made it that much tougher if I needed to go hard confronting one. And the vulnerable, diffident kids could rise to the occasion when they needed to. I just didn't know which, if either of these, Lauren really was.

She was almost to shore. She stood up and leaned for a bush, grabbing it as the boat slid under her feet. She stepped over the gunwale but went sideways into the water, hanging onto the bush, her legs in the mud. I offered a hand and pulled her up. The scrap boat slowly slid down the river. She was breathing hard, exhausted.

I wanted to take charge of the situation as quickly as possible, for lots of reasons.

– I've got you a place to crash that's secure. Just come with me.

She looked, at least temporarily, defeated and open to cooperation.

– Ok, well I guess I haven't got a lot of options at this point. I just need to grab a backpack I hid along the water up there.

She gestured downriver to the north.

– How far?

– Just like, I don't know, two minutes if we can walk there. Took a lot longer by boat. I'll recognize the tree. These guys are ok – she hesitated and looked around toward the tent – really. But ... just come this way.

She was dripping wet but slowly recovering some energy. I followed her.

Suddenly she stopped and turned to me.

– Wait. What are you expecting to get out of this? Like a bottle of water and a minute inside your office is one thing, but I'm not going hiding out with you. And I'm not fucking you if that's where you think this is going. You know I haven't got cash and I can't pay for your help so don't get –

I knew no such thing, actually, but it wasn't the time or place. I interrupted.

– You're right—I'm helping you and it's not free—but all I want is a little information. It might help with an important case.

I was more or less speaking the truth and she could, I hoped, sense it. She turned and pointed.

– My bag's right over there. Wait here one sec.

She disappeared into the brush closer to the river and, after a few seconds, I started to wonder if she had changed her mind or if I had scared her or some combination of those and she had decided to rabbit. Before I could think it through, she re-emerged with a small backpack.

We walked away from the river and reached the bottom of the embankment. She started to scramble up toward the Springwater Trail. I grabbed a strap hanging from her backpack and she spun around.

– It'll be slow, but probably better we stay down here as far as we can. Unless you've settled things with the guys who are after you.

– Uhh... I guess if you say so. And no. I don't even know who those guys are.

Sooner than later I'd need some honest answers, but this wasn't the place for an interrogation. I let it slide.

We had reached the area where the trail and railroad almost meet the river, which forced us up onto the paved track. I looked around and saw no one. More than once, I had toyed with the idea of getting really solid night vision goggles—military grade—but, every time, I talked myself out of the expense. I worked in the city, right? It was never really dark enough to where I'd need them. Then I started thinking about how much gear I could buy using just a tiny slice of the crypto loot Lauren had taken off with...

A chirping sound in the grass brought me back to my task. Maybe I should try a softball question. I needed to build rapport somehow and quickly. Lauren was walking in front, her back to me.

– When did you get into town?

– Just a day or so before I met you at your office. I came down from Seattle.

Ok, that was at least a half truth.

– How was that? Ride down with friends?

The barely perceptible rain that comes and goes most spring days was starting to spin up into a minor storm. I thought about how long we'd be out here and figured on only another quarter hour if we were lucky.

– I was on the Amtrak, it was chill.

Later on I had a lot of painful hours to think about why I flubbed the next bit and, honestly, I'm still not sure. But I definitely flubbed it. I asked:

– Was your brother with you?

Lauren froze and spun around.

– Oh fuck. Fuck this. Fuck this...

She drew out that last word for a few seconds and then darted to my side and past like a frightened cat. She ran toward the river. I spun and followed. There wasn't much land and she'd have to slow down or stop shortly.

Through the rain, I heard the whine of a big electric bike or motorcycle behind me on the bike path. Then voices a dozen yards behind. Lauren was twenty feet in front, and ten feet beyond her was the river.

Four cracks rang out, light pops like a .22. I had a few tenths of a second to be confused before I got hit in the shoulder and realized these were not .22s but suppressed fire from something vastly more substantial. The force half spun me around and I lost my balance. Although it didn't exactly hurt, everything was tingly from the left shoulder down.

I dropped to the ground and pulled my .380. Six more rounds sang out, close enough together that I knew there was more than one gunman. Even with the extra mags, I was equipped for a crook or two at most. I knew I would be vastly overmatched if this turned into a real gunfight. I just hoped if I sprayed enough lead in my pursuers' direction, they might not realize their advantage.

I sent a few rounds towards them, hoping they were equally cheap with the gear and didn't have the night vision it would take to end Lauren and me instantly.

Suppressors hid almost all the muzzle flash, which meant I was firing nearly blind ... but the sound still had a lot of directionality and I dumped my mag where I heard the last shot.

I heard swearing in multiple languages. Then silence for a few. Then more shots. From what I could make out, I had taken one of them out. But that wouldn't be good enough. I struggled to my feet and sprinted toward Lauren, getting to the river just in time to see her on another scrap of fiberglass, a cartoonish manic surfer paddling out toward Ross Island.

More shots cracked from behind me but they were spread out all over the place. I ran as far as I dared using the sound of the gunfire itself to cover my thrashing through the brush. As soon as they stopped—and it wasn't before they had loosed at least twenty-five shots—I froze, knelt, turned, and returned fire. This time I could make out one silhouette against some light scatter, so I made it count. I got at least four of seven rounds into the middle of the guy and he was finished. The rest of my mag was spray and pray. Then I waited for them to reload and start firing into the brush again, dispensed half of my last mag and turned to get the heck out of Dodge.

My remaining shots hadn't hit anyone. And the bad guys had more ammo left. I took at least one more hit before the noise stopped completely.

I was starting to really feel the pain from the first shot but I struggled to keep my breathing steady and stay quiet. I heard two voices. It looked like there had been four of them to start, I had somehow managed to take out two, and the remaining two decided I wasn't worth further trouble now that Lauren had gone her own way. One man fired a few rounds across the water before the other yelled at him and they stopped. Between the river, the darkness, and Lauren's home field advantage, they had to let her go for now as well.

The whine of the electric motorcycles faded.

I looked myself over and I was losing blood like a vampire's dinner via multiple holes. Despite that, I sensed I should worry more about succumbing to some sort of shock from the pain down my left side than about losing consciousness from falling blood pressure.

The world got bright for a moment, then faded to black, then the dirty night returned. No way I'd make it all the way off of the Springwater to where I could ... what? Order a ride? Wait for TriMet to a hospital? Hope 911 could send someone in under a half hour?

There was exactly one other option.

I dragged myself along the edge of the river, northward toward the Ross Island Bridge. There was an encampment: a sort of Freeport for the hobo pirates of the North Willamette. And there was, often, after a fashion, a doctor—well, more of a field medic—of whose services I'd twice availed myself in the past.

Some thoughts ran through my head about Oregon's frontier ethos and how Portlanders seemed compelled—perhaps unwillingly, maybe even unwittingly—to keep it alive. I crawled out of what was now a driving rain and fell face first onto a muddy fiberglass floor made of derelict boat hull.

20

A while later I heard voices from the "bar."

— You should hear the university-level bullshit that comes out of that guy's mouth when he's half awake.

— I try not to...

I attempted to sit up. It hurt like hell all over but I managed it, pulling and scraping at the soggy cushions for some help.

The LED tree lights were still lit but it was day outside.

Eddie wandered back to me.

— You can stay here today. Nothing's going on. If there was anyone following you, they'd have gotten here a long time ago. Last night would'a gotten even more exciting.

He laughed.

I told him I appreciated the offer but I had to get back to work. I had a lot of people to find before I ended up with even more enemies.

— Ok. In that case, I got just the thing for you.

He disappeared and came back rolling a dilapidated wheelchair towards me up a soggy piece of plywood.

— I can push you over to the end of the trail. Where SE Fourth ends. I don't know if there's a bus right there these days...

– I'll owe you... In fact, I'll pay you. And I'll owe you.

I pulled out my wallet and offered him all I had: five twenties. The medical care, such as it was, was free, or recompense for a kind of loyalty. But the transport up the bike path? Eddie was not in the greatest shape himself. He'd lost a foot to an infection already and diabetes was threatening to take as far as the knee.

He accepted the cash.

– I'll use it for more medical supplies, ya know? For next time, right? Although ... if you keep messing with these same guys, I don't know I'm gonna be able to help you next time.

– Well, Eddie, you're goddamn right about that. These guys are pros from a crew up north, international connections. Not my business and way outa my league in a fight.

I felt a little adrenaline and my head seemed clearer. I tried to text Lauren but she had blocked me.

– Ok, let's take this ride.

Eddie got me to fourth and hung around smoking until a car arrived. The look on the driver's face when he saw us was priceless. I think the only reason he didn't take off is he couldn't turn around right at that spot and he was scared of what we might do if he tried to bail. He relaxed a little when Eddie helped stuff me inside and the driver realized neither Eddie nor the wheelchair was coming. I waved to Eddie as the car pulled off.

Staring at the rideshare app a few minutes prior, I had had to make a decision on a destination. My bed was extraordinarily appealing at this moment. Heck, any of the hotels on my circuit would be pretty great and almost justifiable. But I knew where I had to go. A reckoning with Ricardo at 1816 SW Montgomery.

21

I didn't relish the hike from the street in my present condition so I called from the car—to kind of set the stage—and asked for a hand getting up. He said he'd have the gate open and to just drive up to the house.

When we arrived, Talbert was under the porte cochere with a wheelchair—a fancy electric one—and, after helping me into it, he guided me inside, into the cramped elevator, and all the way to San Roman's office.

He seemed practiced at it and shrugged off my thanks. When we got to the office, my injuries must have presented a bit of a scene.

– Was this... – he gestured at me, in the chair – ...incurred on my behalf?

– Yes ... not exactly ... ok, maybe.

Time to get right into it.

– Ara was talking to this girl when she was shot.

I pulled out my phone and opened the album.

– I have reason to be confident the bullets were meant for the girl and not Ara. Any idea who she is?

I cranked up the brightness, zoomed a bit to the face, and spun the phone around toward him.

Ricardo San Roman was an innately expressive man who often found himself in fairly repressed company due to his chosen social circles and spheres of activity. I was expecting the restrained Ricardo but that's not who I got.

First, his eyebrows went up. Then a sharp intake of breath. He held the breath and tightened his jaw. His hands flexed against the surface of his desk with sufficient strength to lift his bulk—easily two twenty-five—off of the floor. He dropped himself and then slumped into the chair and exhaled. His body language was trending more submissive but his brown eyes remained fire.

I thought he was going to scream. Instead, he emitted a strange keening moan which lasted three seconds or so—a lot longer than it sounds. And then he abruptly stopped.

– Lorena.

Now it was my turn to react. In my work, I've needed to learn some skills around emotion and one of them is handling surprise. It's not enough to hide the surprise from others. Just experiencing it internally can distract, leave you vulnerable, and ruin your memory. But there are ways to work around the full strength of a shock, allowing me to function now and revisit the situation later.

He spoke up again.

– My daughter.

Despite those skills and a lot of practice, my head went spinning. I tried to focus.

– She lives with her mother. A good kid. Straight-A student. What did she want from... from...

I waited.

He broke down crying as he sobbed out Ara's name.

I was less puzzled by Lauren's (Lorena's?) having a conversation with her ... what? ... godsister? Is that a thing? But, yeah, I was less puzzled now by that conversation than by the apparent involvement of Ricardo San Roman's straight-A private school kid dodging cartel bullets and buying black market kidneys.

The other shoe dropped. A black market kidney for ... her brother?

Ricardo had stopped crying but remained disconsolate.

– I'm sorry. I'm really sorry. But I have to ask a question here: does Lorena have a brother?

Another moan started up from deep inside the man, slow and soft but building like the whine of a jet engine spinning up and preparing to produce thrust. Then came a full-throated bellowing.

The sore and bleeding holes in my shoulder and back vibrated with the sound waves.

There was nothing to do but attempt to stay calm and wait and, frankly, after the prior twenty-four hours, I didn't have the energy to do much more than stay calm and wait. Something here was outside of grief, though, and a small part of me was sensing histrionics and getting annoyed.

I waited some more. San Roman gestured for me to sit. I was already sitting. In a wheelchair.

He left the room. A minute went by. He came back, having, it appeared, splashed his face with water and his glass with Scotch.

He sat down across from me and suddenly seemed all business.

– I have to level with you about a couple of things. I know it's not smart, or effective, or the best way to work with a professional, what I did, but...

He spoke the word "professional" in a kind of sing-song which, circumstances being different, I might not have let slide.

– Sometimes I have to lie to my doctor, and sometimes to my lawyer and it's the same thing here. It just is what it is.

– Ok... So what is the lie? And what is the truth? I'm assuming you wouldn't mention the lying part if there wasn't a bit of revelatory truth coming after.

– It's like this: Lorena is my daughter. Good kid. Paul is her older brother. Not such a good kid. He's gotten into a lot of trouble over the years. For himself. For me. For lots of people. And he's kind of lost himself. He's not fully together at this point. I've had to be tough with him but I love him of course. When I saw the video of the first attack on Ara, I had this strange feeling right away that I somehow recognized the character and, after repeated watchings, I came around to thinking it was Paul. I knew the whole city was going to be after him, with Ara in the spotlight this week plus the election turning up the heat on everyone. It was awful timing and he was probably high or having a breakdown or both. Sadly typical for Paul these last few years.

You're a sharp guy, you have a lot of connections and you get out on the street where most people don't. So I called in a favor or two because I thought you'd find him. You'd get him to me before the cops got to him. I could get him out of here. Worst case, I could lawyer him up and put him in a hospital in California. If the cops got to him first, he'd be dead. He has no sense, no self control, and, sometimes, a death wish. He'd fight them and he'd be armed. You know how it would go.

I needed to get to him first. You're the best in my book. I was sure you would succeed. Also, I didn't have a lot of other options.

– Ok, ok. I don't like your tactics but I understand the strategy. So, you're saying Paul attacked Ara? Why?

– It's hard to say with Paul. It's... You can't understand what it's like. I've tried so hard to help him. He wouldn't come with me. He wouldn't stay in a hospital. He wouldn't take his meds. But... So... If there was any reason at all, it was probably that he wanted money. Money probably for drugs. He also had some other serious health issues.

I didn't say anything but I raised an eyebrow.

– I couldn't give him more money. And he couldn't get the medical treatment—other treatments—he needed anyway. You have to be clean and meet a bunch of conditions to get on the transplant list. It was never going to happen. It wasn't about the money for screenings. And I'm telling you he would have lost the money anyway, spent it somewhere. You don't know. I pray you don't ever have to know.

I thought about how much to tell him and I thought about what he might still be holding back.

Spilling everything I knew—or suspected—was not likely to be useful. But he had just lost someone close, almost lost someone even closer, and he—and I—were unaware of how long she would last on the run. I decided to tell him a bit about Paul but skip the drug money and secret transplant for the moment.

– I've spoken to Lorena and I think Paul is alive. I'm not sure he's here, though. He was with Lorena in Seattle a couple of weeks back. She's here but he might be anywhere; I have to get ahold of her again.

– She always has her phone. It's –

I interrupted.

– She's blocked me.

– Yeah, she does that. Maybe try Carolina?

I looked on, confused.

– Carolina is their mom...

He was starting to break down again. He slumped on the desk. Stared at a picture of Ara with the woman whom I assumed to be her mother.

– Talbert will give you her info.

He started whimpering, his head down in his arms, against the desk.

Squeezing my chair's little joystick in my fingers, I clumsily, silently rolled into the elevator.

22

I got the info from Talbert and got out of there. Next, I went straight to a pharmacy and bought a crutch. It was 3 p.m. now and I was starving. I took a rideshare home and, from the back seat, ordered a feast from the fancy steakhouse on Burnside for delivery to my apartment. I pulled myself upstairs to wait for the food. It was well over a hundred bucks. That fucker—I thought about the ruse San Roman had engaged me in—owes me. I poured the gin while I waited for my steak.

The remainder of the evening was short and blurry. I awoke a few times due to the pain. Tylenol and Aleve were less effective than the overwhelming fatigue and I managed to fall back asleep each time.

At a bit before 9 a.m., I decided to stay up, grabbed my laptop and went to Nick's Cafe for breakfast. I don't think he had ever seen me order—and eat—so much. After my third order of bacon, he looked worried. Nick had come to the Northwest from Crete in the 1960s at twenty-two, which made him around eighty years old. He'd earned the right to comment on whatever he felt deserved it and anyway I'd been coming here for years, so he began expressing concern for my health in a roundabout way.

– The doctors... They tell me not to eat too much.

He gestured at my plate and continued.

– I try. But I love the stuff. Never ate it back home. *Sigklino* we ate—you would love it. I don't know...

He was clearly considering expanding his menu and my palate to include the Greek pork dish. His wife looked over from the register. Now she was worried, too, though I got the impression her worry was more about mixing cuisines at the very American-style restaurant than about my bacon consumption.

I put them all at ease.

– I hear you about the doctors. And I take their advice. Mostly. Today, I'm recovering from a rough few days at work, that's all.

The wife shrugged. Nick looked at the crutch and turned back toward the griddle, calling out as he did so.

– This town is insane. The town is insane.

I left thirty-four dollars as I got up to head outside. There are places in Portland where that'll get you one beautiful egg in fancy sauce, a hand-massaged coffee and not much more. Nick's is not one of those places. I ate half the menu and left a solid tip with that thirty-four dollars.

23

I walked a few dozen yards and lowered myself into a bench near the old Custom House. Wincing from the twisting action it took to pull my laptop from my bag, I opened it up, not sure what I expected to find. Maybe I just needed to ease into some form of thinking about the manifold situations I was tied up in, and the keyboard and screen were a familiar tool.

I had Lorena to find and her mother's info to bootstrap that effort. Unless ... I couldn't suppress the thought ... she turned up at a hospital or in a homicide report first.

And, apparently, I was now trying to save Paul from himself. But I was hardly closer to finding him than before I knew he was, well, him. That is, when I was looking for a vagrant with a strange walk.

I texted San Roman: "Can you tell me more about Paul? As much as you can. Anything will help."

No immediate response.

I phoned Weatherson at the Multnomah, mostly to make sure he was still there and surviving on the room service. After that, it looked like all roads led to Carolina Ariza—the maiden name of Ricardo's ex-wife, mother to Lorena and Paul.

After a minute or two of pleasantries by phone, Carolina agreed to meet me. She proposed a West-Coast-evolved sort of Italian outfit right where the fancy part of Goose Hollow starts to melt into the even fancier Portland Heights. By some coincidence that likely wasn't, TriMet doesn't serve this area just a thousand yards from downtown. So I jumped in a rideshare and emerged ten minutes later to find an empty dining room.

I looked at my phone and, sure enough, there were about half a dozen messages alternately apologizing and insisting on my accommodation. Something to do with a sick chicken. Carolina invited me to come directly to her home in Bridlemile.

Another car and another twenty minutes brought me to one of those neighborhoods that resembled one-time suburban-dream Los Angeles. Something like Brentwood, long since swallowed up by the city, but still a place where the residents' only concession to reality was a tax bill. And, in exchange for keeping that account current, they expected entirely to avoid the blood, poverty, fentanyl, and general filth those taxes were ostensibly intended to moderate.

Carolina's home didn't comport with the model.

The lawn was scruffy and rural and stood out strikingly on this street of perfect landscaping. The house itself had mid-century modern bones. Simple and small, once a starter home but now—like its California brethren—valuable enough to earn significant upgrades and renovation. Bright spots here and there in the long grass turned out to be dog toys as I approached the front door, which stood open about halfway. I knocked twice.

– Mr. Louis? Come on in!

The interior was dark and warm and smelled of wet dog, chicken droppings, and cat box.

– I'm in the kitchen. Straight back. Hands full at the moment, I'm afraid.

The scent was thick and my breath caught for a moment but it had nothing on day-old corpse and so faded to the background of my consciousness before I made it through the house to the kitchen.

Here, in a sunny spot which faced onto the backyard, stood Carolina. She indeed had her hands full: her right administering some sort of treatment to a stunningly large rooster held in the crook of her arm while the left emptied a container of food into a bowl through the open top of a rabbit hutch. Any rabbits, if present, were not visible.

– Would you like something to drink? There's water on the table.

She gestured with an elbow toward a battered but sturdy wooden dining table which hosted a glass pitcher of yellow cloudy fluid. My skepticism must have revealed itself as she quickly corrected.

– Oh, I'm sorry, that's lemonade. There's water in the fridge if you want. And glasses –

I interrupted.

– Thank you. Please don't worry about it. I'm fine and I really appreciate your time here today, Ms. Ariza. I can just wait if you need a few minutes.

But by then she appeared to be finished, turning to me and wiping her hands on a sage green print maxi dress. I followed her hands down. Despite the chaos and grime, she looked good—I could see what San Roman had liked. Her feet were bare as she strode toward me on the gray laminate plank.

She hopped onto a barstool at a built-in counter ledge and gestured for me to take the other. I hesitated and glanced in the direction of the living room. The living room, which adjoined the kitchen open-plan style, was hopeless: a sofa and armchair piled high with a mix of fabric, yarn, animal toys and grooming knickknacks, two stacks of books, and an ancient reel-to-reel tape deck. The barstools and breakfast nook would suit. I dove right in with a carefully crafted but honest spiel.

– Lorena is in a bit of a dangerous situation right now. She and her father came to me for help and I'm happy to give it. But I've lost track of her for the moment and I really need to find her if she's going to stay safe.

For a moment I wondered if I was in the wrong house. Carolina was entirely unruffled. She bent down to stroke a rabbit which had appeared outside of the hutch—abracadabra!—at her feet. I wondered if that was a studied opportunity to hide a reaction. But when her face popped back up—well, she was either a mighty fine actress or really didn't expect different news.

– Lorena has been mercurial and impetuous for a long time.

The merest hint of a high-pedigree Spanish accent tickled the vowels of her Ivy League diction.

She continued.

– Especially where her father and Ara are concerned. She's terrifically angry with both of them and so protective of her brother Paolo, despite everything.

Her look asked if I knew what "everything" referred to. I figured it was time to come clean with that bit.

– In fact Paul—Paolo—is connected to all of this. Lorena was helping him...

I hesitated for a moment.

– ...to see a doctor in Seattle. They left Seattle together about a week back. I'm not sure if he made it to Portland, but she did and she made some dangerous enemies along the way.

She sighed—naturally, not dramatically—and wiped her hands down her body again.

– Is Paolo ok? His father and I tried everything over the years. Money. Doctors. We tried to call in political favors.

My eyebrows shot up.

– Political favors? Like how do you mean?

– Paolo's dream was to fly. Big planes all around the world. Like 787s. He was training to be a pilot when he failed his first drug test and they kicked him right out. We got him back in. He got his license and was working on advanced training when he failed another flight school drug test. We went all over, pulled every angle to get him back in. You know, Ricardo can be very persuasive.

I thought about how that truth had landed me in the present moment. Carolina continued.

– The school has an air taxi and photo operation for getting more flight hours and Paolo was doing great there for a bit, you know, building up his experience. But at the end of his first year he screwed up and this time he failed an FAA drug test. He was ashamed. Furious. He demanded Ricardo try to fix it with the FAA... But that's way above where Ricardo had any influence. We tried to raise it with both our Senators—you know we did a lot to help them get re-elected—but they threw us out and said if we asked about something like that again, it would be the end of the San Roman family in Oregon politics. And we don't know anyone big in D.C. There's nothing we could do about the flying. Honestly when you see what has happened to Paolo...

She couldn't finish but I had a couple of ideas how that sentence might end.

– I understand, Ms. Ariza. That's really rough. We've had trouble like that in my family too. And in addition to getting Lorena to somewhere safe, one of the reasons I need to talk to her is to learn where Paul is. He's in danger himself.

– I don't know what I can do...

– Would Lorena take a phone call from you? A text message? She blocked me in anger when she stormed off. I had let on that I knew about her helping Paul out with the doctor, but I didn't manage the timing of that reveal real well.

– She's been ignoring me too, I'm afraid.

She looked off into the distance across the backyard, where two small goats walked around in a large pen. Conflict knitted her brow. I waited. Finally she spoke, softly, almost whispering.

– How serious is all this?

Was she that out of it? If she didn't already get it, I needed to be clear.

– It's life and death, ma'am. Those bullets that killed Ara? I'm nearly one hundred percent confident they were meant for Lorena. And there's more. A few –

She interrupted me again.

– There's one thing I... A few months ago I overheard Lorena with her friends. She set up a second SIM in her phone—like a second number. You can do that now. She doesn't know I know about it and I've been keeping it ... secret ... in case I ever need to reach her. Once she knows... But I'll give it to you.

I was encouraged but also unsure how to gently yet quickly extricate myself from this conversation afterward; luckily, a goat needed to be fed. Carolina texted me the number and walked me partway to the front door before heading out back to the goats.

There were a lot of hours left in the day and, despite lingering annoyance at San Roman, I was feeling energized in a peculiar way by the information I had been learning. My mood was further improved knowing I could get at least one message through to Lauren/Lorena. I took a rideshare to the waterfront so I could get in a short walk and do some thinking on the way to the office. I made my way north along the river and then took a left and crossed into Old Town.

24

I offered a smoke and a light to two bums sober enough to stand up outside of the comfort-food cafe at the base of the Multnomah. I hadn't seen these guys before. They were friends and both smelled of sweet pipe tobacco. One of the men looked alert but didn't speak at all. The other immediately introduced himself as Pete. He held the cigarette in his left hand and slowly dug his right out of a beaten military field jacket worn over at least two layers of flannel. The hand was calloused, blistered, scarred, and filthy. But it had none of the telltale lesions of the local drug culture. That got my attention a bit.

Pete and his buddy had hitched from Alaska—or so they said—and were thinking of heading to San Fran. They wanted to do some fishing here in Oregon, though, first, if they could find a little work.

These men reminded me of a Portland gone not too long ago, born rough, of steamships and sawmills. A Portland we'd vigorously chased out for spotted owls, *Portlandia* and Silicon Forest dreams. Suburbs got some microchips, a brief shot at the upper-middle class. The city entered the Upside Down, a nightmare from which it couldn't wake. We got heroin, then meth, then fentanyl, tranq, mayhem, murder, and an ironically well organized pile of anarchists sworn to prevent anybody's doing much about it.

I pointed out a dealer on the corner of Burnside, then invited the men to follow me instead. My office was halfway to the bus station and, while I hated to say it, they'd do well to leave town while they could still function.

Pete smiled, two broad gaps in his yellowed teeth. He started to speak when the silent friend cut him off with a first utterance.

– Thanks, but, like my friend said, we're here for some fishing.

The friend's mien was more hostile and I realized it was time to move on. I gave a feeble salute and headed across Burnside to send a carefully worded text message.

I proposed the song-and-dance that had worked with Weatherson: the Nines and a disguised passage to the out-of-service wing in the Multnomah. To my surprise I got a read receipt and a message right back.

"thx - rly! am safe for now tho n better stay put a bit. maybe if things heat up?"

If things heated up ... well, it didn't matter. The next move would have to be Lorena's.

I wrote back.

"ok - text anytime"

At least for now, it stayed on unread.

Not great, but things could be worse.

I turned the corner and approached the building housing my office. Things were worse.

There was glass sprayed across the sidewalk and into the street. Chunks of wood lay on the ground. Bent, blackened metal bits protruded from the door frame area.

As I got closer, I could see glass inside as well as out and similar destruction to the inner door. The digital touchscreen call-box was a brown charred stump.

I had seen things like this once or twice on insurance cases: this was a bomb.

Stepping through the mess, I drew my gun and carefully looked around inside. Nothing on the first floor. Stealthily, I climbed the stairs and peeked across the mezzanine landing. All quiet. Up to the second floor, where a scene of destruction at my office door awaited me. This one looked like a fire axe or battering ram job. The sparse waiting room was tossed and the inner door was missing entirely; two hinges stuck out from the side jamb.

My inner office had also been thoroughly disarranged, the desk emptied of its valuable content—that is to say, of the liquor. The safe, a cannonball salvaged years ago from the Spalding Building for the price of hauling, was unscathed. It had turned out to be more than a novelty, after all. The history of that safe contained traces of twentieth-century Portland the way that a tree's rings bear stories of fires, droughts, and lean times across the years. I mused on its history with our lost local banking institutions as I walked around and verified the office—and building—were entirely empty.

The Portland Trust Company of Oregon was born in 1887, with Henry Pittock (that's Pittock Mansion and *The Oregonian* Henry Pittock) as vice president. Pittock seized control in 1910 and restructured it to create Northwestern National Bank.

Fast forward to the 1960s, and the Commercial Bank of Lake Oswego joined, birthing The Oregon Bank. The 1970s saw them add Security Bank of Oregon, hitting thirty-five branches, and, by decade's end, nearly fifty.

In '87, Security Pacific Bank swooped in, only to be swallowed by Bank of America five years later. The old main branch, tucked away in the Spalding Building on SW Third and Washington, was sold off, a relic of the past as new headquarters rose. The fixtures were mostly sold or discarded but the cannonball came home with me.

The iron showed some light scorching but was otherwise untouched, as were its contents: digital records of all of my work, including a ton of evidence that ought never to become public.

The safe also held the keyring I'd need to open the metal door at the top of a half-flight of stairs above the fifth floor landing. That door led to the roof, the one place I hadn't cleared in my quick pass through the building. I realized I'd better have a look just to be sure.

After exiting that metal door, another half flight and another locked door opened onto the roof. I stepped out and saw no one on the tar and gravel surface. I walked to the edge and looked down. Nothing. Around all four sides, nothing. Then I turned to go back down and saw it.

Painted in red letters a yard high across the roof bulkhead:

END LUXURY CONDOS. ABOLISH RENT. FUCK SANROMAN. FREE PDX.

I was on the phone to the cops when San Roman called. I told the dispatcher I was ok but had to go and then switched calls to Ricardo.

– Jack! Help me god dammit! Get over here and bring the cavalry! There's a whole gang going –

A loud cracking sound came across the line and he cut off.

Someone was dialing things up and it really didn't look like the cartel operators' style.

25

I called Sergeants Berkson and Atkins, plus Detective Whidby, as I headed down the stairs to the street. Two patrol officers were stepping out of their ride as I exited the vestibule straight through the demolished front door.

– I was coming in to work—my office is on two—and this is what I found. Take a look at my office and also up on the roof. Someone left a message. I gotta run but you know where to find me.

I handed them one of my cards with my home address stuck to the back courtesy of charities drowning me in labels.

They started asking questions. It was like a reflex and they couldn't help it.

– Sir, about what time did you –

I needed to call a car and I didn't want to get stuck here in an interview. So I waved and sprinted toward Fifth where I knew one bus or another would get me at least to Pioneer Courthouse Square.

A vehicle arrived and I jumped onboard without even knowing which bus it was. The square is a fixed-point attractor for the vector field called TriMet, which is a fancy way of saying you can randomly hop buses and you're guaranteed to get close.

The bus ground down the street and I quickly cross-checked relationships in my head.

What did San Roman and luxury condos have in common? Prominent entities in the modern Portland architecture and planning scene, connected via Ara, I guessed. And, of course they were both flashpoints in the long struggle between the radical "Portland for the People" scene out of the East Side Kremlin versus the "People for Portland" mindset passing for center-right. So was this really political? If so, what the hell did I have to do with any of it?

If it was political statement season, then making a wreck out of the week's major conference event would be more in keeping with the local style than blowing up some dude's decrepit discount office in Old Town.

So the political link felt a bit off.

At the same time, what did real estate and architecture have to do with Lorena, Paul, drug money, Weatherson, and a cartel? Ricardo San Roman was the only thing in the center of this Venn diagram, but that meant little. In a smallish town like PDX, San Roman and his ilk were in the intersecting circles of every Venn diagram.

I stumbled off the bus by the Pioneer Courthouse three minutes later and walked a block to the rideshare I'd ordered during the brief trip. Ten minutes' drive in a crimson electric sedan felt like an hour. I considered having the driver stop a few hundred yards short of the San Roman property in case

I needed some stealth, but decided against it: Ricardo's call asked for speed not subtlety. My instinct proved accurate when we arrived at the front gate, which had been smashed open. I asked the driver to go up to the house and he complied, unaware we were entering a crime scene, with crime possibly still in progress.

We got within fifty yards of the house when our path was blocked by an old white Ford pickup parked across the driveway. It appeared to be empty. Beyond it was a black Chevy Suburban which might have been occupied. The windows were tinted.

I jumped out, told the driver to take off, and crouched behind one of the wheels of the Ford. If someone had been watching, it was pretty unlikely they'd have missed my red ride pulling up. But the Ford put me out of their lines of sight and of fire momentarily while I planned my next move. Scanning the remaining one hundred eighty degrees in case there was someone covering the rear, I had to hope whoever knocked down the gate didn't know about the four security cameras on the entrance.

As the red sedan receded down the driveway, a deadly quiet settled. Maybe whatever happened here was over already? Given the trend line, that was not an encouraging thought.

I crouched and counted ... fifteen seconds ... thirty ... sixty. It felt like hours. Another full minute ticked off. I half rose, the top of my head barely clearing the hood of the pickup. Instantly three cracks—the shockwaves from supersonic bullets—surrounded my head and I reflexively dropped to the ground.

Now I could see a pair of feet on the far side of the Suburban. They were running up and into the house.

What were the odds that was the only person I'd need to deal with? Weighed against the urgency of Ricardo's message and the clear disorder at the property, I'd have to take my chances. I sprinted to the entrance under the porte-cochere. The door was wide open.

I stuck my head in. Nothing.

Then I heard a scuffle behind me. I spun to see three figures in all black. One was right in my face, swinging something long at my head. I dodged. He swung across my body and I took it in the ribs. The blow was from a pipe or a metal baton and it stung like hell. My broken ribs would hurt more later but in the meantime I saw the pipe fly downward and then around and overhead.

In the split second before it came toward me, I decided to go offensive and lunged straight into the midsection of my attacker. He wasn't wearing anything protective aside from a few layers of clothing and he felt surprisingly soft and weak as I pummeled his gut and drove him backward to the ground. I heard the pipe drop from his right hand and clatter to the floor just as I felt a sap fortifying his left clock my ear. I slumped down and braced for a stronger blow that never came.

The soft man in black joined his associates at the back of the Suburban, where the door was open. I dragged myself along the ground, far enough forward to see what they were doing there. They—together with a fourth person, also masked and all in black—were struggling with a pair of legs protruding from the vehicle.

I couldn't get close enough to see inside or even to spy the face that went with the legs. But when I saw the buttons on the sport coat above those slacks and caught a reflection off of a cufflink, I was pretty certain the haberdashery was that of one Ricardo San Roman.

The Suburban was already rolling. The rear door slammed shut. I drew my gun but had no shot at all. Just as the SUV reached the bottom of the driveway, it swerved onto the grass and I heard a sound like crumpling aluminum foil.

A few seconds later I was upright and watching the truck disappear as one PPB Ford whipped past the property and took off after it. The other of two PPB Fords that had just arrived on scene was now sporting a partly crushed rear right quarter panel earned unsuccessfully attempting to seal the driveway.

I called out to the officer who had exited that vehicle and was running toward the house. He waved me off—he wanted to take a look inside before stopping to chat—and I was in no shape to give chase. When he re-emerged a minute or two later, I filled him in. He made a radio call from his packset just as three more PPB Fords pulled up on the street below.

We were all a few steps behind. From the radio calls, I could tell the Suburban had successfully eluded, with contact lost somewhere in the southwest hills.

It was dusk. It had been a more than full day with barely a rest after getting bullets put into me by drug gang executioners. Bullets which then got extracted in a mildewy trash heap at the edge of the river.

I felt like morally I ought to drink a lot of coffee and spend the night looking for San Roman but my body and mind just weren't going to cooperate. In any case, what I mistook for superego was, on reflection, just his older, domineering brother: my ego. I felt like I had been fucking up. It happened plenty, but I really didn't like when it was so obvious to my clients.

In any case, I wasn't going to make more progress as a solo operator—even if I were in the best possible condition—than the PPB, the sheriffs, the state police, and whoever else was coming in on this together. San Roman was exceptionally wealthy and well connected by Oregon standards so local agencies were already treating this like the Lindbergh kidnapping.

I headed home and checked up on Weatherson one more time—partly to reassure myself that I hadn't lost everyone I was trying to keep tabs on—then fell into a deep slumber.

26

Everything hurt substantially worse when I arose the next morning just after nine. The second and third days are always the worst. Ask me how I know. I brewed some tar-strength coffee and slumped down with the laptop.

Exactly one message stood out.

Hey Jack,

I've got your attention I trust. We need to talk. 11:00 a.m. at Liberation Lounge.

– Billy

P.S. Sorry about the office. Once things got going, we just couldn't help ourselves.

Who the hell was Billy? Who was "we"? A few searches turned up zilch on the Liberation Lounge. Maybe it was new, or newly renamed?

I could ask around but I wasn't feeling big on energy. The heck with it, I thought, and hit reply. I didn't commit to the appointment but did throw my ignorance out there.

"Sorry, but I don't know where that is. Do you have an address?"

And about a minute later, I got a response.

"200-block of SE 15th. Look for the umbrellas. Come all the way through, I'll be in the garden out back."

Now that I had an approximate address, I thought I'd find out more. It didn't take. In fact, based on Portland property maps and USPS, it didn't look like the place even existed. Of course, whatever was there was blurred on Street View. That should have been my first warning, but lots of places are blurred on Street View. I had to admit I was intrigued.

After a long hot shower and more blistering black coffee, I gathered my gear for a possible ambush and set up one timed message to Sgt. Berkson and another to my lawyer. If I didn't cancel it in four hours, at least someone would know where to search for the corpse.

27

I took TriMet out to southeast a half hour early for recon. I circled the block. The neighborhood had a tight mix of commercial as well as residential streets, with spots of quasi industrial here and there. It looked like 200 was a residential block but that wasn't a huge shock. It was common enough on the east side to find the odd coffee shop, bar, sandwich-and-kombucha counter, or hobby bookshop embedded right into a shed or garage on the same lot as a Victorian.

The Liberation Lounge didn't appear to be a coffee-and-beer nook, though. At the spot which the online map had blurred, the sidewalk was bordered by pruned and landscaped rose bushes. Sun shone on a low grassy embankment and a broken concrete walkway led upward to a hulking Craftsman-style house painted red with black trim. There was no sign for a business, but two black umbrellas mounted in the ground flanking the walkway matched one over the front porch—a subtle and unnerving sort of branding.

I walked up to the house, climbed four wooden steps to the porch, and looked around. The windows were all covered with curtains; the front door was solid except for a peephole. I didn't see or hear anything. Walking to the edges of the porch, I could see that a high brick and stucco wall wrapped the side and back yards. Even with the height of the porch under my feet, the top of the wall was another three-plus feet above my head.

I thought about knocking but decided against transmitting any unnecessary signal. I delicately felt the doorknob. It spun loosely in my hand—as though it were not connected to anything. Nevertheless, with light pressure, the door swung inward. It was massive but balanced, maybe even counterweighted. No latch elements—bolt, strike plate, et cetera—were visible on the door or frame at all.

Inside was a short, pitch-black hallway. Beyond the hallway, a red, lit room was visible—or at least a red painted wall. A voice called.

– Go ahead. Close it up and come on in.

I stepped in and pushed the door closed behind me. Electric solenoid locks clicked all over the place. Unusual security, but it explained the doorknob.

I emerged from the short tunnel into one of those homey coffeehouse-cum-bakery-cum-pub sorts of places. At the counter stood a tall thin man in all black save for a blue surgical mask, green earrings, and white nail polish. A glance around revealed one patron in similar garb seated by a bay window. The window didn't add much light, since it was covered by shutters on the outside. The man was drinking something that looked like tea from a pint glass.

Both men looked at me but said nothing.

I started tentatively.

– I'm here to meet a guy named Billy. He said he'd be in the garden so maybe…

I gestured toward the back of the house. The man at the counter nodded. I heard heavy footsteps behind me.

– Just a second, my friend.

Two more men started patting me down from behind. They were rough and quick but knew their craft. Within ten seconds, they relieved me of my gun, utility knife, zip tie flex cuffs, phone, and pepper spray. I couldn't swear it but I think they felt for wires and cameras as well.

The barman offered an uncanny-valley grin.

– No need to come here armed. We're the friendliest people in all of Rose City.

He placed my belongings inside a metal locker at the end of the counter, snapped a lock shut, and handed me the key. The wall behind the lockers was decorated with a couple of gas masks and a Guy Fawkes mask.

– You'll get it on the way out… Unless… You're not a cop, are you?

The patron with the tea interrupted the procedure.

– If he were a city cop, we'd know it before he did. Every damned one of them is in the files. And their pets, kids, allergies, the color bike they got on their tenth birthday.

His pride was visible.

– Unless he's a fed…

I stopped the exchange by answering the original question.

– No, I'm not a cop. A private eye, that's all.

The tea drinker opened his mouth again.

– Could be a fed. Would never admit to it alone and out of uniform. Cowards.

One of the men who had frisked me spoke up from over my left shoulder:

– Unless he's under real deep cover, he's just a shitty private snoop. Has an office in Old Town. Well – here he theatrically stifled an exaggerated laugh – *had* an office in Old Town.

I was surprised he knew about that. Maybe I shouldn't have been.

– News travels fast.

– Yeah. News.

He and his compatriot of the slick hands guffawed and the man behind the counter affected a bored and annoyed pose. He pointed toward the hallway I had come through when I entered.

– Over there. Go through, turn right, go all the way back. Billy's in the garden.

Another solenoid clicked and a door slipped open in the side of the darkened hallway.

I pushed through it, turned right, and walked through a long dim hallway toward a bright green sunlit patch at the end. Twenty-five feet later I emerged into a tiny backyard beer garden decorated in *Lord of the Flies* stake-pig.

A pudgy man of thirty or so in black hoodie, black shorts, and a black vented Covid mask sat in an Adirondack chair with a laptop on his thighs and a beverage in an Imperial pint glass on the armrest.

He gestured toward an identical chair at a one-hundred-twenty-degree angle to his.

– Ah, sit! You must be *Jacques Louis.*

He spoke that rendition of my name—one I'd only ever heard from the mouths of my grandparents—with an exaggerated and silly French accent.

– You're *tres fameux* around these parts.

He giggled then suddenly sobered up. Pulled the mask up a bit to take a sip from his glass.

– Sit down, Jack.

He glanced back toward the hallways by which I had entered the garden. Reflexively, I looked as well. Now there were four men standing there. They took a step forward.

I sat down.

– Ok. Billy, is it? Who are you and what do you want?

From the direction of the house, music suddenly started playing. "Singing in the Rain" blared from a Bluetooth speaker.

– Well, first I want – his voice shifted to a scream and he turned toward the men behind him – a little bit of fucking quiet and some privacy! Get the fuck out of here and turn off the goddamned music!

At least two of the men sniggered but the music stopped and they all disappeared inside the house. The door shut with a heavy click. I thought about the twelve-foot-high brick and stucco wall. This place was quite a little fortress. Or prison.

– People say we have no sense of humor. That we're dour and depressed all the time. But you know better now, don't you?

I told him I didn't follow.

– Never mind, Jack. We're just two ships passing, really. But I'm going to need your help with just a little... Jack, you need to do something for me.

I waited.

– I'm going to have you get five million dollars in Bitcoin for me and send it to this address...

He pulled a folded index card out of his pocket and handed it to me. I took it. I was utterly confused.

– Where would I find five million dollars and why would I give any of it to you?

He nodded toward the index card. I opened it. On it was printed what appeared to be a Bitcoin address. And below that was taped an Oregon driver license. That of Ricardo San Roman.

– You take this and get with his lawyer and with Carolina and with Lorena and with whomever else he... Never mind. You've got twenty-four hours.

He was getting emotional, agitated, and louder.

– Maybe not even twenty-four – you'd better hurry. Five million isn't a lot these days for people like him. He'll be getting off easy and I swear to god he knows it. His lawyer will give you the five mil by dinnertime.

He was breathing hard, hyperventilating or struggling with his breath. He tore the mask off completely. His voice came out louder but also unevenly, warbling, almost cracking.

– It's nothing for what he's done. For the things he and his people have done. To ... to Ara, to me, to ... to this city!

I wanted more information and to be asking more systematic questions. I had a pretty good idea now what I was dealing with here—Billy himself was a wildcard, but the rest of these jokers... I fought back the strong temptation to grab this smug self-satisfied little clown and squeeze until the revolution lost some appeal.

An alternative approach was called for. I spoke deliberately, decelerating the pace of my words as I went.

– Ok, ok. Let's just talk for a second. You're holding the cards and none of this is my business anyway. I'll take this to Ricardo's lawyer and if what you say is true, he'll set wheels in motion. But...

His eyes lit up. He took a big swig of his beverage. I went on.

– What is this even about? You act like you know me, but who exactly are you?

He thought for a moment then pulled down his hood, pulled off the mask, and dropped it.

– Hell with it. Who am I? What is this about? I'm Billy. I bet they never told you one word about me. I'm Ara's fucking brother! Well, half brother. The wrong half, isn't that what Ricardo said the one time I got to see Ara after our parents died? After his kind of people killed them, really. Christmas at that monstrous tumor of a house. Of course I didn't understand anything about it back then. It was like a castle. I was just a little kid. The house was magical. I didn't understand a lot of what was going on but I could tell Ricardo was being very, very witty when he said "the wrong half" in front of everyone at dinner. Ara went to live there, her new house in the new year and become "Ara San Roman." I didn't make it back to Portland after that until twenty-fucking-twenty.

I gave the most interested-empathetic-therapist look I knew how. Anything to keep him talking. As it turned out, he had a lot bottled up and seemed to be gaining momentum.

– You know, I would have been looking at Portland grant proposals in D.C. Deciding what we would do for this city. And what we would demand in exchange. I was going to have a full-time gig at the Future Rights Campaign, a decent apartment in Foggy Bottom, not the upper bunk in a rat-infested room share... Anyway, they shut it down. Covid. Sent us home. My colleagues went to places like Ricardo's to spend the pandemic eating lobster and drinking champagne and paying lip service to Black Lives Matter. There was nothing for me. I had to leave town, drove back to Amherst. Crashed with an old prof for a month until his wife kicked me out then I drove around the country living in my car. I got as far as Eugene before the engine seized. I probably should have changed the oil. Or at least checked it. I started rethinking the advocacy life. I think these guys here have a more meaningful approach.

He gestured around the garden.

– Or at least a more effective approach. Sometimes you just need to burn things.

He finally stopped to breathe. It was my turn to get agitated but I knew I had to keep it under control.

"Burn things" was a bit close to home for me. Gwen Farmer—most locals remember her from channel seven news—and I had been friends since 2001. We worked on some of the same projects. Helped each other through a lot over the years. Then I got to visit her in the hospital—sometimes daily—for months after the thugs shot rockets at her news crew. The TV station was setting up to report outside the mayor's condo while Billy's gang were busy trying to burn it down. A firework rocket exploded in a trash can. There was oil or something inside. The fire sprayed and stuck to the whole crew but Gwen got it the worst. She was out of the hospital early 2021 but that was it for her career.

Except maybe on Halloween, they'd never put her anywhere near lights and a camera again. She didn't have a lot of options after that—the story was a problem and, back then, no mainstream news org could hire her. The FBI took all the evidence and never let her lawyer have a thing. She got a more expensive lawyer; the city said there had never even been a trash can in that location. She lives with her mom in a trailer near Yreka and sends me drunk texts from time to time. I've tried to explain things are different now but she's long since given up.

My anger rose. I still had a wire utility saw hidden in my belt and ... deep breaths. Deep breaths. It was not my turn for drama.

I tried for something anodyne.

– So you went to Amherst?

– Not Amherst the school. I was at Hampshire. Same town though.

– It sounds like things went well there.

– That's kinda true. It was really great and that's how I got internships at True Peace Coalition and the gig at FRC. Future Rights Campaign—they call it FRC. But it was all a bluff, sort of. I mean I was as legit as could be. But not like the other kids. Inside I wasn't the same and everyone could tell. At some level they could tell. You know, I never saw Ara after that Christmas? I'm sorry, I know this is confusing. I'm a little upset. But you ought to know who you're really working for. I'm still going to get the five million.

– Ok, I hear what you're saying. Ricardo adopted Ara and not you?

– Pretty much. I don't know what happened exactly. I was young. I had to go live with my uncle.

– And that was a rough life? Not a good family, you had to work your ass off and go into debt...

– No, that's not it. It's not like Dickens. Actually, maybe it is a little like Dickens. Different book. But anyway my parents had a million dollar life insurance policy and Ricardo didn't get much of it despite trying. My uncle was pretty nice, the family was great, really. The money was a lot back then. I had a bimmer in high school for god's sake. The money covered going to Hampshire. Even had a hundred grand or so left over when I moved to D.C.

I gave him a quizzical look but kept it gentle and open. I didn't want to risk shutting things down. Or prompting an extreme reaction.

– When you hear it like this, it sounds like I had it easy. But it's the principle of it. It's not justice. Ricardo became Ara's father and so now she ... so ... she's this big architect and designs the city. That was supposed to be me. Well not exactly. You know what I mean. It's not fair. But. It's gonna be ... well, more fair. Go take this and get me my five million dollars.

He stood, pulled up his hood and put the mask back on. Gestured toward the door I had come out of.

Story time was, apparently, over. But I had learned more than I'd expected. I walked to the door, heard the solenoids click, stopped at the front counter with my key to retrieve my gear and silently walked out the front door and down to the street.

I walked around the block one more time just to think and observe. I was walking west on Pine toward 15th when a garage door flew open and a silver '90s Honda with no license plate, a ton of scrapes, and a modified low rider suspension pulled out—about fifty feet in front of me—and turned west, then stopped. The driver and two passengers were all in black, with hoods and masks. They appeared to be arguing with each other.

What were the odds? I asked myself, ducking down and trying to get closer to their vehicle before it took off. I was damned curious where these fine fellows were heading. Especially if one of them was Billy.

Without a vehicle at the ready, my options were limited, though. I stayed low to the ground, scrambled up behind the Honda, and stuck a tracker under the bumper near the exhaust. These clowns all thought their opsec was Bond level, but the only reason they weren't locked up years ago was the grift pipeline. The political and union arms of the group had bought their friends sweet jobs at the Central Courthouse—in the legal offices and also on the bench.

The tracker would buy me some time, but not enough to go dig out my car. I had contact info for some enterprising rideshare drivers who offered to help me out, so I started with Kareem. He picked up on the second ring and offered to meet me at Pine and SE Grand in five minutes. I thought I could just about do that running, told him so, and got to trying.

28

I was watching the blue dot of the location tracker due south of me near the Ross Island Bridge when Kareem picked me up. I called out hasty directions and we turned at Ankeny to get on MLK going south. The Honda appeared to be cruising down 99E with just five minutes' lead on us.

The tracker wasn't a GPS device, but one of those mesh-network gadgets you can use to find your stuff, and the location got laggy and spotty as they left the congested stretch where we were still sitting in inner-east-side midday traffic. By the time things opened up for us on McLoughlin Blvd, the Honda had popped a couple of times, most recently near the Clackamas River. If they got too far out of town, we might be out of luck.

We were cranking down 99E at about sixty when the blue dot snapped and stopped moving a bit before the bridge where I-205 crosses the Willamette. Now the game was hoping they didn't go too far from the vehicle before we could catch up. We got roughly abreast of the dot and I had Kareem pull over so I could jump out.

He smiled and waved his phone.

– I'll send you a bill. A big bill.

I smiled back and laughed. In this era and this town a help-ful driver was worth almost any amount.

– Yeah... not too big this time. Please.

He pulled away from the curb and I started half-stalking, half-running, taking in the street scene, keeping an eye on the phone map, and trying to move quickly. The car looked to be two blocks away—west, near the river—on the digital map.

Heading that direction brought me along a chain-link fence past a narrow weedy yard filled with a mix of parked boats: nice looking if slightly neglected vessels on trailers, along with a few unlikely ever to sail again not least because of the black-berries growing through tears in their hulls. Next, I crossed a gravel parking lot at the end of which a slate-gray building with a cracked translite—"Beer as cold as the Willamette!" (fea-turing a smiling, foamy, wide-eyed and anthropomorphized mug)—promised refreshment, lottery games, and bingo. A neon sign, unlit and difficult to see against the tube's backing, read "Falls Pub."

Immediately next to the door of the Falls Pub was the silver Honda.

I wouldn't have called this place for an anarchist bar, I thought, as I swung the door open and dove into the darkness. And I was right. The boys in black were nowhere to be seen and the decor was so Americana it could've been Alabama.

Behind the bar was a heavy man with a puffy white beard. And, under his hands, on the bar, was a Mossberg Cruiser.

I took a deep breath, made sure he could see my hands, and as softly as I could manage asked whether he had, by any chance, recently seen some young men dressed all in black exit a silver car outside his door.

He replied enthusiastically, lifting the barrel of the shotgun toward the ceiling as he did so.

– Damn right I did. I hadn't pulled this old boy out in a decade.

He waved the gun.

– Those sons of bitches piled out of that car, one of 'em opens the door and takes a step inside here. The one with the face like a human tackle box and the commie tattoo. Behind him, his buddy's got two pieces of rebar or something. And there was another one who hadn't made it inside yet. I looked at the first asshole, racked the gun and told him he and his pals had the wrong address and probably the wrong goddamn county. Right outta the Portland retard factory, these kids. Least they had the good sense to turn around and leave without openin' their mouths.

– Any idea which way they went?

He gestured to the west and down with the barrel of the shotgun.

– That way—the gravel road to the river. Tripping over themselves running – he laughed once – and I'm about to have their car towed, matter of fact.

I nodded and grinned.

– They should have parked somewhere else. I appreciate the info.

Just past the bar, a long gravel road led down to another lot, some launches, boathouses, and a few other buildings hugging the base of the cliff. I followed the road down, not liking how exposed it left me, until I could get behind some barrels and a jersey barrier near the bottom.

I looked around—there was no one visible and numerous candidates for hiding spots: boathouses, a couple of small buildings like concrete bunkers, some metal sheds, and a fuel-and-bait shop that appeared to be all shut up.

I slowly advanced, staying close to the cliff, hoping to find footprints in the mud areas—anything, really. It was pretty hopeless. But I had caught some luck and, as I made my way through the gap between two rows of small metal sheds, I heard a man cursing loudly from the direction of one of them. It had once been whitewashed and was mostly rust now, with a power service mast sticking out of the corner, where three stubs of cable poked into the air.

There were no windows or doors on the side that I could see. Circling the building revealed no windows and a single, sliding sheet metal door in the north wall. Grunts and muffled squeals emanated from the gap where the metal door met—but did not seal with—the opposing section of wall.

I approached and maneuvered to squint through the narrow gap.

A set of white fluorescent tubes illuminated a group of men, all in black, beating another man who sat in the center of the shed secured to a chair. A piece of filthy linen covered the head and shoulders of the man in the chair and the muffled squealing emanated from there.

A number of tactical problems had to be resolved before I could act. Despite the lit interior, it was still bright outside; without pressing my face to the gap, my eyes were underexposing. Due to the angle, I couldn't see the entire interior of the shed—so I didn't know who else might be inside or what they might be armed with. The sliding metal door was on a rusty track: I couldn't count on a quick move throwing the door wide—even if it wasn't secured shut, a door like that could take a lot of force to slide and even then move slowly. And, on top of all that, I didn't know if there was someone standing guard elsewhere among the sheds or boathouses, ready to come at me from the rear.

Events got ahead of my ratiocination. From a corner of the interior—where I had not been able to see—a man walked toward the chair and yelled at the others to cut it out. The yeller removed his hood. I recognize him as Billy. He removed the hood of the man in the chair. It was a fairly bruised Ricardo San Roman.

One of Billy's compatriots started up again, screaming at San Roman.

– You know you don't give a fuck about what's right! You know you need to give something up to fix things!

Billy interrupted.

– You owe me a fucking apology. And a lot more than that.

The crony poked Billy in the shoulder and got in his face:

– Drop the bourgeois family drama. This is about the city and about the world!

In a less tense situation, I think I might have burst out laughing. But if there was humor here, it was too dark for that. The crony swung the rebar and made contact with Ricardo's head. A moment later blood was coursing down over his ear.

I had seen a total of four men aside from Ricardo. I hoped that was everyone because I only had twelve rounds in my pistol and it was time to stage an intervention with this dysfunctional family.

I drew my gun and placed my foot on the edge of the sliding door—to keep my hands free and also to bring more weight to bear if needed. Applying sudden force to the door didn't move it freely but did get it all the way to the stop, leaving a four-foot-wide opening between me and the avant-garde theater rehearsal inside.

All the men turned. Time slowed down. Billy stayed next to Ricardo but the other three came at me, two with aluminum baseball bats and the nearest to me with a machete. I immediately opened fire. My gun barked four times before machete man collapsed. The other two attackers froze. I stepped to the side and tried to keep them both covered.

– Get the fuck out of here! – I yelled. It was as close to negotiation as I was going to get before opening fire a second time.

Billy and one of his pals accepted terms and dove out through the open door. The other man seemed to be following but, after one large step, turned toward me and swung the baseball bat at my head.

I ducked as I fired another three times. One of the first shots must have hit his neck: blood sprayed the wall before he fell to the ground gurgling and coughing.

I pulled out my own knife and started cutting Ricardo free when I heard movement behind me, coming from outside.

Two men I hadn't seen before—dressed and equipped like legit tactical operators—moved in. One of them had Billy and his accomplice cuffed together. He was dragging them to their feet using a pain compliance technique. The other man thrust the butt of a close-quarters short carbine into my chest and knocked me against the wall of the shed where I slid to the ground—which was already covered in a layer of blood—trying to catch my breath.

He grabbed San Roman, cuffed him, and pulled him through the doorway behind his teammate. Right before exiting, he pulled a telescoping baton from somewhere on his ensemble of gear, snapped it out, and smashed the two lights in the overhead fixture.

I aimed and fired repeatedly at this man to absolutely no effect. He was sliding the door shut. My magazine was empty. This guy was either superman or—more likely—wearing decent body armor. The door closed and I heard the sound of a chain sliding. The door tilted a bit, nearly sealing. Two heavy clicks sounded. It was not entirely black inside but close to it. I slowly started to get up. When I got to the door and listened, all was silent. I was secured in the shed with two dead anarchists while some pros had made off with Ricardo San Roman, Billy,

and the most fortunate—relatively speaking—of Billy's associates.

29

I wondered for a moment whether the rust in the shed walls was so severe that I could just kick a hole and climb out. Then I remembered I had my phone in my pocket so I called 911 and told them I needed Oregon City PD like now. Mostly to account for the bodies on the ground ... but also to cut me out. I told them to bring bolt cutters and also an angle grinder, just in case.

I tried not to—as they say—"disturb the crime scene." Mainly I needed to preserve things because the Oregon City cops didn't know me. And I didn't have any influential friends close by, so when OCPD set eyes on this mess they would have to play it as it lay and go slow.

It would probably work to my advantage that the bloody corpses on the floor belonged to the MultCo visiting team and wore the uniform. It was a point of pride throughout Clackamas County to never roll out the red carpet for these guys.

Looking at my phone, my other loose ends were coming looser. It appeared there had been a dustup of some sort at the Multnomah Hotel and Weatherson was now gone. Of his own volition or not was as yet unclear.

And Lauren had seen fit to communicate saying only that she wanted to talk in person, somewhere in town and in public. I'd be at the Multnomah anyway—provided things worked out with the local cops—so I asked her to meet me there at 5 p.m.

When the cops arrived five minutes later and finally got the shed open—they had needed the angle grinder after all—daylight streamed in on the horrific sight.

The kid who had taken the bullet to the neck had donated well over a gallon of blood to the concrete floor, and more than a little of it was on me. The police carefully pulled his mask off. Looking at him, I honestly felt awful.

He was really young—maybe twenty?—and had probably started out legit protesting injustice, lost perspective, and got all torqued up with these jokers. But the outcome here wasn't funny at all. They planned to save the world by destroying everything as the first step and—as in every cult and every revolution—were getting played by older, bigger assholes who knew better.

I spent some time doing a police interview on site. Then got a ride in the backseat of a cop car to an office building where I spent a couple of hours telling them everything that led up to the scene by the river, omitting only the background that Weatherson had shared: Lauren's drug money, Paul's medical treatment, and the downstream assumption that the people after Lauren were cartel ops.

The least believable part of the story was the last-second abduction from the shed of key characters by the tac-ops guys.

But things weighed sufficiently in my favor: clearly, I hadn't chained myself in the shed and locked it from outside; a solid account of my credibility and a passable account of my recent work had filtered in from Portland and MultCo personages; and CCSO was already pointing to a right-wing group that constantly tried to skirmish with Billy's buddies.

After repeating everything in yet another recording for another pair of detectives, they called it a day and even drove me back to the Multnomah. I got there a few minutes before five, grabbed a coffee, and looked for Manny to give me the scoop on Weatherson.

Alexa, the day-shift manager, a late-twenties goth-dye-brunette sporting a proper Portland level of ink, told me Manny would be in at six. I waited for Lauren.

30

She never showed.
I texted and called her on both her numbers and got nothing.

It could be that she just flaked again. It could be bullets caught up with her. It could be something in between.

I shifted gears when Manny came on duty. He had a bit of a tale for me around Weatherson.

– I'm embarrassed to admit it, Jack, but we … none of us had a clue until it was too late. We got a call from another hotel guest saying they had heard what sounded like a fight in a neighboring room or the hallway. Figured it was usual drunken nonsense, and radioed our patrol officer who was just checking the parking garage. He got up to the guest rooms in question just four minutes later—it turned out it was probably Weatherson's room making the noise: the door was propped open on the security latch, the room was empty, dark, and partly trashed. Occupant gone. We didn't find anything in the property—stairwells, garage, other public areas. Looked at the security tape and two guys had dragged Weatherson out through the main elevator, lobby, and west doors before we even got to the room. Here: check out the tape. They look like pros.

I watched the recordings. The men reminded me a lot of the guys who had grabbed San Roman and Billy and locked me in the shed. No way to know if they were the same guys, but it almost didn't matter. The similarity and close timing had to be more than coincidence.

So someone had now grabbed Weatherson, San Roman, and Billy. Maybe Lauren as well.

At this point, I was fried, not to mention absolutely starving. I thanked Manny for everything and wandered out into Old Town, fantasizing about ever-more-enticing dishes as I considered my dinner plans.

31

I drifted, half stumbling, unconsciously, until I was looking through the plate glass on SW Third Avenue into the front dining room of Huber's.

Huber's is Portland's oldest restaurant, best known for serving turkey and for keeping the lights on since 1879. In other cities, a place like that would be a novelty tourist attraction, cliched even as simulacrum, like cloying theme park "Main Street" Americana.

Instead, Huber's is what it was. As such, it foiled any search for a credible phase transition from past to present. The streets of Old Town, where Huber's is located, were some of the earliest to see their mud replaced with cobbles. That project—rather like the restaurant—remains ongoing. Numerous blocks with a credible claim to being downtown remained dirt and gravel late into the twentieth century. Some are still that way today. In Portland, to paraphrase a famous Cascadian, the present is here just not very evenly distributed.

In fact, the era didn't much matter as I watched the cooks cranking out platters of turkey at an absurd rate. There was so much steam that the bottom half of the window was covered with condensation on the inside.

Before I could step into the place, my phone rang with a video call from Carolina Ariza.

I wondered if maybe—just maybe—it was really Lorena. After all, no one my age starts video calls on purpose, though accidental dials were not entirely unheard of.

I ducked into the corridor that runs parallel to the front dining room and leads to, among other places, a modern rarity: a stunning, windowless internal dining room complete with stained-glass skylights. A touch brought the manic if haggard face of Carolina onto my screen. I fumbled with my earbuds but she was already talking.

– I need you to help me with something!

Well, hello to you too, I thought. And wasn't I already running all over Portland, getting shot, almost hacked in half, and who knows what else trying to help her family? I didn't give voice to any of that, though.

– Well...

I took a breath, made myself look even tireder and hungrier than I felt, and spoke slowly. Tactics to get a touch of control over whatever exchange was going to happen next. I continued.

– Let's see... What can I help you with, Ms. Ariza?

– Paul needs help. Lorena said he's in trouble. Hollywood. Just off Halsey in a garage... Lemme see where she said...

I jumped in.

– You've spoken with Lorena? When? She was supposed to meet me tonight and never showed up.

– Oh. No. I just got a text. Umm... The cops were gonna take Paul somewhere but instead he let them contact Lorena and he promised he'd go with her.

– So that's where she went?

– No. She couldn't go. She sent me this and said to please go help Paul because she couldn't get there.

– Did she say why? Or where she was?

– No. But it must be serious. She has always dropped everything to help Paul, risked everything she had. Over and over no matter what. Also, she said she was losing bars and couldn't text anymore. Now that I say it out loud that way, maybe she was in trouble too. Well, more trouble.

Now? Maybe? I didn't say that out loud either.

– Is there anything else that you can tell me? That she said? And ... doesn't her phone have that fancy satellite messaging thing?

– I don't know about any of that. I'll send you screenshots of the messages if I can get this thing to work. There isn't much else. Oh. It was 41st and Halsey, there's an abandoned store there with an underground garage and Paul would be hiding in it.

– Ok, ok. But. So, I apologize for asking it this way, Ms. Ariza, but... Why aren't you going to help your son yourself? I mean, I understand the history, but it sounds like he's in extremis.

– Oh, yes. I would. I mean, I will. But it will take some time. See, the baby goats need to nurse, or to be fed if they won't nurse. They're very delicate at this age, so... I'm sure you understand.

This woman was beyond scatterbrained, past eccentric and unusual, flirting with dementia and various mental illnesses. I could feel myself, exhausted and hungry, being pulled along, losing focus. Is dementia a mental illness? There was an argument both ways. Oh my god. She was getting to me—I hoped it was just the fatigue. I'd have slapped myself hard if I weren't still on video.

– Got it, Ms. Ariza. Don't worry. I'll go look for Paul and I'll let you know if Lauren—Lorena—ever turns up at the hotel where we were supposed to meet.

– You were meeting Lorena at a hotel? Do you know how old she is? What

If I hadn't been so tired, I'd have burst out laughing.

– It's my job, Ms. Ariza. You know, the one where we're trying to keep Lorena alive long enough for the cops or the DEA or whatever cavalry is gonna come to the rescue?

As I said it, I realized I hadn't quite spelled out the details of the girl's situation to her mother. But, I told myself, if her mother were even a part-timer in the here-and-now, she'd have some idea what was up. After all, Ara had made the news in Budapest by this point. Twice.

– I feel so silly, Mr. Louis. So silly.

– Don't worry about it. I'm gonna go get my car and have a look for Paul. I'll let you know what I find.

I disconnected.

The hallway was full of the smell of Huber's turkey and Huber's ham and Huber's stuffing and ... I wasn't going to be having any of it tonight.

I felt around in my pockets for a chunk of protein bar while I stumbled onto the 15 bus to go get my car. Things were moving too fast now to rely further on transit or even rideshares. Not to mention, any place without a cell signal—any place Lorena might have been dragged off to—wasn't going to be on a TriMet frequent-service line.

32

The growl of an idling Mustang must be the same thing you'd hear if you put your head against the chest of a vigorously purring lion. A sub-bass so deep it rumbled every part of your body, even while the decibel level stayed subdued.

I tried to keep my foot light on the pedal so as to keep a pretense of stealth ... or at least decorum ... as I wheeled out of the garage and down the block.

Already, the kinetics and acoustics were combining to make me more alert. As I hit the Vaughn Street ramp to I-405, I dropped the hammer and crossed the river with that 435-horsepower grin—wide as a dinner plate—and no verbal thoughts at all.

I eased up on the throttle to make the tight turn onto I-5 South before dropping to the surface streets right past Broadway. The mind still boggled at Carolina's peculiar predilections and priorities, but who cared: I was triple-dipping on this particular mercy mission. Sure, I was helping Carolina. But it might also get me close to solving the original assignment and saving Paul from suicide-by-cop or something equally ugly. On top of that, Paul was the closest recent contact to Lauren

I knew of. And the gang claiming title to "Lauren's" drug money were looking good for the recent abductions.

Another ten minutes and I was wheeling through the smashed-open fence surrounding a shuttered department store. The parking lot was covered with everything from take-out bags and fast food wrappers to orange-and-white syringes and scraps of foil. In other words, it wasn't too different from Chinatown east of my apartment. The underground lot was less a traditional rectilinear parking structure than a sort of dugout cave with a sloping entrance and exit. I remembered that much from when I had bought an electric shaver here in another time. The garage was also absolute darkness—like staring at Vantablack dark. I parked amongst the McDonald's cheeseburger wraps up on top, pulled my flashlight out but didn't illuminate it just yet, and headed toward the chasm.

I didn't hear anything, but then the traffic on Halsey would guarantee that.

Slowly, I walked down the ramp, looking for any sign of movement. I didn't see any and I didn't see Paul either. I was about to say the heck with it and yell out his name when I saw a flicker of flame against the wall about forty feet from where I stood.

I called out—to anyone who might be doing anything down here:

– Hey... Are you ok? I think I lost my jacket down here. I've got a cigarette if you want one.

It was a sort of diplomatic protocol.

I heard rustling as I slowly approached where the flame had flickered. My light was still off.

A hoarse voice softly called out.

– You got anything to eat, man?

The answer was, technically, yes. But I wasn't sure that was the play. Instead

– I got a flashlight. Is it ok if I turn it on?

– Go for it, I guess, but don't put it in my face, ok? Please?

I lit the beam and dialed it to the least extreme level of blinding, pointed at asphalt and then slowly panned to the wall near the voice.

The reflected light revealed a grimy young man lying on an equally foul blanket. His face had an uncanny and nauseating sick look. But there was something a touch unusual here. His overgrown hair and moderate beard had no trace of gray. Face mottled and crusted but not wrinkled or sun damaged. And his hands, arms, and—especially—his bare feet showed nothing of the usual sores, cuts, and infections that quickly mark those living on the street. Either he was preternaturally resistant to the rough life or he hadn't been here long at all.

Moment of truth time.

– Paul?

– Hey! What the fuck, man? Who are you?

– Your sister and your mom sent me. Let's get outta this spot, ok?

– How do I know you're telling the truth?

– I know your real name is Paulo. And your sister is Lorena. And Ara is your step-sister. And –

– Yeah but anybody knows that. What about... what about... I gotta think.

He paused for a good fifteen seconds and I waited.

– Ok, what kinda pets does my mom have?

– Well I know about the goats and the rabbits... is that what you mean?

– I guess. Wait. One more if Lorena really trusts you. What's her beef with Ara?

This one stumped me. I didn't even know there was a beef. If I knew the details, that might contribute a ways toward unraveling this tangled situation. But for now I had no hope of bluffing.

– That one I don't know. I'm sorry. She never mentioned it and I never asked. Trust me. Let's get you out of here.

He hesitated for a bit then hauled himself to his feet, using the wall as a support.

– I guess it doesn't really matter anymore.

Behind the blanket was a trash bag which he grabbed. I swung my light toward the ramp I had come down and slowly stepped in that direction. Paul followed me.

We got to my car and I silently thanked God I had the leather interior and not the fabric. I opened the door and helped him in, his bag in front of him under the dashboard.

– Can I take you to your mom's house?

– Oh shit, no. Not like this. Not. I mean, can we get something to eat first? I haven't eaten anything all day. Yesterday I hit the Whole Foods on Sandy and grabbed a feast. They didn't even hassle me. Maybe we can go up there. I'd kill for some meat or vegetables. And some beer. It's just too bad they don't have any real booze over there.

I thought for a minute, did a little planning and optimization, and had an idea. There was a dirt-cheap motel right around the corner here on Sandy. And up the road a pace was Clyde's.

– I have a better idea. Let's go get you a room right here at the Block Orchard Motel. You can get a shower. Maybe I can find some clothes somewhere.

– No, I got my clothes. Right here.

He slapped his fingers against the trash bag between his legs.

– Ok, ok. So you can wash up and get dressed. And we can get dinner at Clyde's. I'm starving too. We'll get a couple of nice slabs of meat and a proper drink.

Even in the relative darkness I could see his eyes light up and a smile widen across his lips. I noticed teeth that also looked way too good for someone even briefly on the street. Until recently, he had somehow managed—with the help of his sister—to keep himself together. I guess I shouldn't have been surprised, but his parents had me thinking things were worse. On the other hand, it made sense: Weatherson would never have risked operating on someone who looked street-level fragile.

We drove the hundred yards to the mostly empty Block Orchard where I rented a basic but clean room for less than we would pay for our prime rib.

I sat on the bed and flipped through channels while Paul showered and washed up. He did have a decent set of clothes in the bag along with another smaller plastic bag containing a razor, toothbrush, and the like.

The first thing I'd need to find out is how he had arrived in such straits.

While he was showering, I noticed the room was made up but there was no blanket, just the sheet. I poked around looking to see if a blanket was stored in a drawer. No joy.

I called out.

– Paul! I'm going to go to the office and find a blanket for the bed, or you'll freeze later when you get back. You're not gonna take off on me, are you?

He seemed in better humor when he replied.

– And give up prime rib and some drinks? Are you crazy? I'll be right here.

I went to the office and, after a few minutes' delay, received two freshly washed blankets. I headed back to the room.

Paul was just finishing cleaning up and, although he might not pass in the Clyde's dining room, he would be no problem in the more dimly lit lounge.

We drove the 'stang the mile up Sandy to the windowless faux-stone edifice that was Clyde's Prime Rib. Nodding to the hostess and receiving a nod back, we took a booth opposite the bar.

33

Paul was keen to order some hard drinks and I wasn't going to stop him. But I made sure we got a ton of water and bread right away. If he got drunk or violently ill or worse, there were potentially a lot of lives at stake. I needed what info he had.

A mentor once explained that the word "I" is the favorite out of all of 'em for most people, and if you let them talk, they'd pretty soon talk about themselves. As a corollary, if you let them talk about themselves, they'd often talk about what they knew—or thought they knew.

I put that advice into practice and started the interview by shutting up. Once Paul had eaten half a loaf of bread, drunk a quart of water, and a cocktail waitress had brought two large gin martinis, my approach yielded results: Paul started talking.

– I don't know how you know my sister or mom. You never really explained that. But I guess I'll take your word for it.

He paused to slurp his drink and I thought he was waiting for me to explain. I got ready to summarize the situation in a minimally upsetting fashion but didn't get the chance. He resumed:

– It was funny you didn't know the thing about Lorena and Ara and the cat. I swear everyone in my family knows the truth, they just don't want to talk about it. I guess the real problem is they feel guilty for lying about it back then. Coming clean and admitting that part now would be the worst. I dunno. One time I had a therapist convinced me maybe—just maybe—they didn't know what happened and they were just trying to... No, never mind Lori's cat for now. Yeah. I'm the only one who gets to call her that, you know...

He had to stop for a moment. The same waitress had come back over and took our dinner order. There was some magic in the Clyde's prime rib ritual: for just a moment, as we were ordering and talking about it, the waitress, Paul, and I all felt a wave of happiness that mixed contentment with excitement. We had silly smiles talking about the meat. The waitress walked away and things got darker.

I thought I might engage in a back-and-forth at this point, but no. Maybe it was the recent trauma or the loneliness of the street. Paul kept on with a sort of disconnected monologue.

– Let's just get down to it. Lori and I are both in a ton of trouble now. Lori took some money to help me and the people whose money it is, they got to us fast. Hit us both before we even got out of Seattle. For my part, the doctors up there did an amazing job, but I've got an infection now. I wanted to keep a low profile for lots of reasons. Picked up the strongest antibiotics I could get on the street, but they didn't work. I gave up and got into a street clinic two days ago. Beautiful doctor—man, you should have seen her—a Russian, I think. So hot. But she said I had to get into the hospital or I'd die. She was going to have me transported. I took off. I'm still moving but barely.

He laughed a little bit.

– Lori's in the shit too. They got her. She told me about you, said you tried to help. I don't blame you, ya know. She thought they were going to shoot her right away but at the last minute they just bundled her up and threw her in the trunk of a car. Phone and everything. She told us both—me and the cop who called her. I think the cops are going to look for her. They have to, right? I mean, they have to do something...

– I don't know what they all told you about me. I don't really blame them anymore for not helping me. I mean what's the point now? And I know I fucked things up for them. I used to be really angry—I thought the public embarrassment for my dad was the only thing he was really upset about.

– I'll tell you what, though. I'm not stupid. As soon as I found out what Lori had done, I tried to talk her out of the whole thing. Told her to give the money back. Even after the surgery, I told her to give back the rest of it, and we'd figure out the medical stuff, deal with Weatherson somehow. That guy doesn't impress me. I think after they came at her so fast in Seattle and shot the place up where we were crashing, she was open to ideas, but by then it was kinda too late and... Like really too late. I heard Ara died. That's also because of me. I don't have anything against Ara anymore. I thought at worst it would be me and Lori paying the price.

I had to take the opportunity so I cut in abruptly and firmly.

– Paul, then why did you attack Ara?

– You mean like why did I cause trouble with her and dad in the old days?

– No, I mean last week when you beat her with a bottle. You might have noticed you made the news and, thanks to the timing, they talked about you in Paris and Berlin.

– What the fuck are you talking about? Why would you think I was that guy? That's insane. Hell, when that went down I was in Delta Park unconscious in a tough dude's camper. I think I know where to find him and he'll tell you.

– I saw the video. Your dad saw it. The way you walk—a family thing with your hips?

– Really? Jesus Christ. My goddamned family. Some lunatic walking funny so you all decide it's me?

When he put it that way, I had to second guess San Roman's conclusions. It was possible, maybe even plausible with the hip disorder, but I couldn't claim it was likely. Maybe this was the issue Ricardo foresaw with the cops? Then again, none of that really mattered now.

– Ok, look, it's like this. I'm not sure about anything except that your dad hired me to get you out of trouble. He thought it was you, or at least he told me that, and he said he didn't want the cops to find you. He wanted me to find you instead, said he could get you to California or somewhere, get you some help.

– Funny how he suddenly wants to help me after Ara gets hurt. Lori said something about that once. Well you can see how well he helped me up until now. But it doesn't matter. I mean this might literally be my last meal.

He paused and showed a wan smile.

– Not a bad one… Hey, you've got that car and you said you were here to help me tonight. Want to really help me?

I wasn't sure where this was going. I just said, "Ok."

– Take me to the airport. Not PDX, the little airport—Troutdale—where I learned to fly. Lemme just take a look around there one more time.

We had wrapped up with food and I was paying the bill. What the hell, right? The man's dying and all he wants to do is see a few acres of asphalt twenty minutes away?

Sure, I said.

We left Clyde's and got back into my Mustang.

34

The roads were empty. And Paul seemed to enjoy the roar of the V8. So we were parking near the fence on the north side of the field inside of fifteen minutes. I had done a little flying out of Troutdale myself, so I didn't mind a chance to walk around the place a bit even if there wasn't much happening in the evenings.

The FBO lobby was open but the only one there at the moment was a security guard, an older white man with a stringy beard. Paul, looking somewhat respectable and emboldened by gin martinis, immediately introduced himself as a former student—technically true—and asked to go walk around the planes.

– Well, the books are all locked up in the office – the guard gestured to a closed wooden door – but you can look around I guess.

The guard was referring to the binders with aircraft keys and documents. Paul headed toward the flight-school aircraft tied down outside.

I walked a bit closer to the taxiway and sat down on a bench to watch traffic on approach to PDX. After a few minutes, I picked up a landing light that seemed to be on base for the runway at Troutdale. I watched it approach and, as it turned final, I glanced over in the direction of the tied-down Cessnas where Paul had been.

He wasn't visible among the planes but a red aircraft beacon light was blinking over there. I squinted and started walking closer. I saw a silhouette through the plexiglass of a 172 window.

He must be on the far side, I thought, when I suddenly realized that the silhouette lacked legs. Paul had gotten into the plane.

The guard must be new to aircraft, especially single-engine planes going on fifty years old: although they had locks and keys, locks were often worn out and had never represented serious fortification to begin with. Over the years, lots of repaired magneto switches and starters didn't even have locks, just toggles or buttons.

I started running in Paul's direction. I waved and called out.

I got closer. The tie-down chains were still in place. Theoretically he shouldn't be in the plane, but maybe he was just enjoying a moment in the left seat.

A few seconds later, I neared the pilot-side door. A figure was slumped forward. I pulled the handle and the door popped open. An unmistakable smell hit me and I reflexively coughed, retched, and stepped away. I shined my flashlight into the cockpit where the beam hit Paul, completely unconscious and bent over the control yoke. Moving the beam down illuminated the source of the smell: a glass straw and a piece of foil with some substance burnt to blackness on its surface.

I looked around. The only light was the FBO. I sprinted over, swung the door, and called to the security guard.

– Where's your first aid kit? You have Narcan handy?

Most places in Portland did.

– Are you kidding, son? This is a general aviation airport. Not much call for that around here. What's going on?

– That man I came in with—he's passed out in one of the planes. Looks like he hit the fetty and too hard.

– The control tower is open—you could call there. Maybe it's in their kit. Or else just call 911. The sheriff and fire are plenty fast getting to here.

I remembered the kit in my trunk.

– Ok, can you call 911, tell them we have an OD here? I've got Narcan in my car and I'll take a shot with that.

I ran around to the parking lot, retrieved the whole first aid kit, and ran back to Paul in the Skyhawk. I got him out and onto the ground and administered the Narcan.

Nothing.

He wasn't breathing. No pulse at all. Not good.

It wasn't unheard of for someone to revive after four or even five doses of Narcan. Problem was, I only had the one.

Turning back toward the FBO, I was ready to dial the tower on my phone when I saw EMS and fire pulling onto the apron. The paramedics went to work on Paul while I recounted the story to one of the firefighters. I think I was mainly getting some stuff off my chest: the firefighter, who saw worse every shift, remained nonchalant. He didn't know who Ricardo San Roman was and, realistically, why should he?

After a few more minutes the EMS crew rolled a stretcher over and prepared to load Paul. I approached and the paramedic recognized my raised eyebrow.

– I'm sorry.

– Nothing?

– Asystole. Um, flatline. We'll keep working on him and get him to the hospital but—he gestured to a handful of Narcan dispensers on the ground—at this point, he's gone.

I thanked everyone on the scene as they closed doors and prepared to roll. And I apologized profusely to the security guard. Poor judgment on my part even coming here, though I was loath to admit it lest some lawyers and insurance companies decide to fight over my near-zero bank balance.

The lights faded away. The security guard said not to worry about it—emergency operations and drills at the airport are important and they'll use this one to learn how to do things better next time.

The words didn't help much. I had been involved in the loss of another of Ricardo's children and the only saving grace was Ricardo didn't know it yet ... if he was even still alive.

I took the Mustang back home and didn't exceed the speed limit the whole way. With no energy to stash it in Slabtown, I left it on the street for the night and stumbled upstairs to collapse.

35

I forced myself out of bed at 8 a.m., the time I had set on my phone, even though I felt about as tired as I had when I'd gotten under the covers. As soon as I recollected my situation, a broad wave of nausea added itself to the exhaustion and residual pain inhabiting my body from the week's prior conflicts.

By this point in an investigation of any kind, the goal was to have eliminated most of the degrees of freedom and narrowed the search space ... a fancy way of saying: eliminate all but a couple of possibilities. That was kind of ... sort of happening in this case, but largely due to more and more key personalities getting kidnapped or killed. Not the way it's supposed to go. At this rate, I joked to myself, soon I'll be the only one standing so I might as well head down to SW First Avenue and turn myself in.

Billy's gang no longer had Ricardo San Roman, so that ransom demand was moot. Nevertheless, I intended to bring the message to his family attorney, Jeffrey Spencer and attempt a wider conversation about the prevailing situation. Mr. Spencer would have to decide for himself what might or might not be proper to share with me. He'd handled numerous incidents for the family over the years and knew where the bodies were buried. There had to be something in all that which could help.

On the surface, it was a matter of finding the cartel operators—if they weren't back in Canada or overseas by now and the hostages weren't all dead. That's not the kind of thing you can clue out from the family stories. But odd and incidental trivia could yield surprisingly valuable sparks and all the more so when the trivia are the only clues to hand. For example, Paul was insistent that he had not attacked Ara in the incident that had started my involvement in this whole drama. He was near death. He might have been lying, perhaps to improve his posthumous standing in the family. But I didn't think so. And if it wasn't Paul, was it a random coincidence and Ricardo was so emotionally distraught that he misidentified his own child in the video? Was there another sibling out there with the hip defect? Besides ... I hesitated almost not wanting to finish the thought: besides Lorena? Was that possible?

That was the sort of thinking which might be clarified in a conversation with the lawyer and might somehow make a difference, though I wasn't yet sure how.

It was a blustery and bright early spring morning with partial clouds but no rain ... yet ... when I headed south from my apartment. Mr. Spencer's firm was located in a 2000s-era highrise close to Director Park. He didn't try many cases so he'd almost certainly be in the office. If not, I'd go down to the river and get him during a recess. That didn't end up being necessary.

Jeffrey was a tall man with an owl-like face, white close-cropped hair and thick monobrow in a gray suit and brown tassel loafers. He gave an awkward smile and reached out his hand. I had met him before and always been charmed by his curious mix of self-confidence and self-consciousness. And, as ever, I reached out so he could nearly break my hand with a handshake.

His voice always boomed.

– Jack Louis!

One had to boom back.

– Jeff!

– It is great to see you! You're looking good!

– You as well but I wish it were under better circumstances.

– Things are looking up. Or hadn't you heard?

– Heard what?

– This is about Ricardo, right?

I nodded.

– He's ok! He's in the hospital but he's gonna be fine! He was dumped off outside of the hospital in Gresham. We were notified just half an hour ago. Whoever took him either changed their mind or got smart about whom they were holding on to.

– Is he talking? What about the others? Billy, and –

– He's ok but completely sedated for now. He was the only one they found at the hospital. They looked around nearby. Frankly, I've dealt with Billy many times over the years and in my opinion it's just as well if he never turns up again. Come on into my office and let's talk. Want a coffee?

I followed the tall man back past his assistant's desk. He rubbed her shoulder as he walked by. The decades had been steadily moving the line between harmless flirtation and sexual harassment leaving Jeff's habits to hang farther and farther over it. But I also knew he was probably showing off for my benefit and his assistant, Amy, was a well-paid part of the act.

I closed the office door behind me and we sat down in two armchairs diagonally opposite Jeff's desk and computer. We looked out the window at a view which impressed whenever it wasn't a picture of winter's white sky. Today, it impressed.

I was almost giddy with relief that Ricardo was free. It was the first decent news I'd had in what felt like forever.

– Regarding Billy, and just so I can do what I said I would, here's a Bitcoin address.

I pulled out the slip of paper and handed it over.

– Billy wanted five million sent there, back when he had San Roman and was planning torture and forced confession whether he got the money or not.

– That kid. He's only gotten worse. It's a peculiar case.

Jeff told me the family's side of the Billy story and it wasn't much different from my imaginings. It tied up a loose end but didn't add anything. At the end of the day, Ara was her mom's kid and Billy wasn't. Then Ara was Ricardo's kid and Billy wasn't. Despite all that, Ricardo had helped Billy and things went fine until they didn't and it turned into the sad but common toxic Gen Z admixture of societal critique and mental illness.

– About Ara... I was with Paul last night.

– Yes, Carolina told me. That too is deeply tragic although not entirely unexpected.

– Jesus, is there anything that you don't know before I do?

– If it's regarding the San Roman family, I should hope not. I'm not awful at my job, you know.

Jeff grinned and waved his arm across the window, a slightly cartoonish gesture meant to have the office's stunning Mt. Hood view vouch for the capabilities of its occupant.

– Ok, ok. So there's this one thing. Paul didn't know if he should trust me. He made a big deal of asking if I knew about Lorena, Ara, and the cat. What is that about?

– Just one of the many San Roman dramas. About a dozen years ago, when Lorena was a little girl and Ara was a teenager, Ara supposedly ran over Lorena's cat at the edge of the road, at the bottom of that long driveway up to their house.

– On purpose? By accident? What do you mean "supposedly"?

– Lorena told everyone that she saw Ara run over the cat. Probably by accident? Ara had just learned to drive. Lorena didn't accuse Ara of doing it on purpose at the time. Ara denied it all, said someone else must have hit the cat, and most of the family insisted Lorena made the story up to cause trouble for her sister. This was, of course, before all of the security cameras. There were no other witnesses.

– Are you saying that, later, Lorena claimed Ara killed the cat on purpose? And that family members took sides?

– Sort of. So the only one who believed Lorena from the beginning was Paul. She and Paul said it was an accident. It's one of those cases where the coverup is worse than the crime. It was everyone else's insistent denial around the whole thing that drove Lorena crazy. Maybe she got over the cat but she never got over being called a liar by pretty much the whole family from such a young age. Things got worse over the years. Later, she often lashed out and accused Ara of killing the cat by design, but I don't think even Lorena believed it. It's just ... the stuff that happens. You know what it's like with a kid and their pet. Something sad happens with that, there's gonna be emotional damage and then with a wealthy, eccentric family... Well, anyway, that's the story. Maybe sheds some light on the Lorena, Paul, and Ara relationships.

– Hmm... I'd say it does. So it's not entirely implausible that Lorena, having gotten herself and Paul into serious trouble pulling off this transplant when no one else in the family would help him, that she might confront and even attack Ara? Especially if they needed more help and got the blow off once again?

– It's plausible. I mean if it had happened at a garden party or behind closed doors, it would be among the more extreme incidents but not a complete outlier when you've known them almost thirty years like I have. It's the downtown MAX platform thing right during the design conference that blew this up. We tried the usual but there was no keeping it under wraps. Too much press. I was the one who told Ricardo to get you on it, by the way... Of course, he was sure it was Paul.

– One other thing. Ricardo dismissed it but I have to ask: this guy they called Magenta, a drug boss from years ago that

Ara's mom and Ricardo helped lock up. Any chance he's looking for revenge in all this?

Jeff's face made a sort of half-grin.

– Nah, I don't think so. First, no one really called him Magenta. It's just that he had a bunch of aliases, some unlikely and some, ahem ... inappropriate for extensive use in public documents. So the feds actually gave him the Magenta moniker. Everyone in that investigation got a color. I think the agent in charge was a big Tarantino fan. Ya know, like "You're Mr. Pink"? Anyway, he's been under the radar for ages, at least since Ara's parents died. Rumor is, he runs a camp in BC that trains commando sorts of enforcers for the cartel, but, if so, he's probably more of a classroom teacher now—he's almost as old as I am. He got stopped in Washington for speeding a couple of years ago. Hey, I'll have Amy print out what we have, including pictures, so you can see what he looks like.

– What a mess. So where do we go from here? The clock is ticking for Lorena. And for Billy, although I'm not sure I care about that angle so much.

– These days, you probably know as much as anyone about... Wait. There's one other person who might have info on Billy. Ever heard of Carrie Gavaghan?

– Carrie Gavaghan... She runs one of the nonprofits in Old Town, right? Tapping a thick vein of taxpayer gold without much to show for it and running her mouth at city council?

– Yep, that's the one.

– What's she got to do with this?

– So she's still got a law license and when Billy and his wrecking crew occasionally get pinched tearing the place up, it's her number that's written in waterproof marker on their forearms. On the off chance the DA is in a mood, and Billy doesn't get released right away, Carrie's a warm body with a bar card and that's enough for a lot of the judges to indulge their deep and abiding sense of social justice.

Jeff's voice was rich with a pungent irony-sarcasm mix.

– She's gotten the same couple dozen kids out of felony charges more times than I can count. And Billy is her favorite. Because he's smarter than the average bear and even paid her actual dollars once or twice. No matter what kind of chaos breaks out, she always seems to know where he is in time to prevent him from seeing the inside of a cell. Sometimes her presence is enough to keep him from taking a ride in the first place. I'll bet you some good Willamette pinot she has access to his location through his phone or a tracker tag or something.

– Good Willamette pinot is overpriced. Does that make it more or less of a wager? Anyway, if we suppose that the ops who took Ricardo and Billy were part of the crew after Lorena, and that they got them all in one place...

– Yeah. The cops are already looking. Even though they let Ricardo go, he was too high profile to not draw attention. And Lorena's only seventeen, so the FBI is starting to spin up too. I don't think any of them have the Carrie angle though—she's a true believer and won't talk to them at all, even to save her own client. Why don't you give her a shot?

36

Carrie Gavaghan thinks of herself as a rebellious, free spirit. Keep Portland Weird and all that. The odds of finding her in her own office were small. I phoned her organization and played it as neutral as I could, said I was trying to help one of her clients.

Discipline in keeping my mouth shut through the years had been tough but the long game occasionally paid off. This was one of those occasions. Carrie knew that I associated with people who were less sympathetic to her causes, but she lacked any concrete evidence of severe antipathy.

I was talking by phone to one of her assistants, a young woman with a reedy voice. Carrie always seemed to have a substantial staff doing other things than what her org was getting financed to do ... and that, I thought, was a trick I desperately needed to learn, especially with the renovations my office had recently enjoyed.

Carrie, the assistant told me as she typed and texted, was testifying before the county commission this morning but would be done shortly and was willing to meet with me. No coffee shop date, though. She would be checking in with clients on

Hawthorne underneath the bridge between Water and SE Second and I should go look for her there.

I wasn't in any position to negotiate so I thanked the woman and wandered back to where I had parked my car the previous evening.

The Mustang was so bright it almost fluoresced in the sunlight and I considered making an entrance under the bridge with V8 roaring. I thought better of it and drove over to the Multnomah County Building garage to ditch the car.

37

I walked west underneath the bridge approach, through remaining bits of inner Portland's industrial zone. This was where the freight trains run, day and night, horns blaring in the rain and fog. Moving oil. Still moving timber. Heard but remaining unseen even to locals, who mostly crossed overhead on elevated roadways and rarely wandered between the East Bank Esplanade and SE Third Avenue.

Carrie was holding court in the midst of four tents alongside a blanket-fort-style structure made of tarps and furniture pads lashed to a frame of bike parts and shopping carts. Nearby, a pile of scavenged electrical and industrial refuse burned on the street, oozing sludge and emitting an acrid smell tinged with ozone.

When I approached, she waved to her clients and they scurried out of sight. She moved to the edge of the camp, up against a corrugated metal warehouse wall. She wore a leather jacket, a variety of metallic accessories, black jeans, and leather boots. A common Portland style anywhere; at commission sessions, only minimally less so. She also wore a half scowl and greeted me by name.

– Jack. Louis. Your name comes up a lot in documents, usually assembling so-called evidence against desperate and innocent clients of mine. I'm sure you're proud of your work.

The voice dripped venomous contempt.

– Are you going to insult me all morning or can we talk about working together to help one of your sometime clients?

– This "help" doesn't involve the police, or health services of some kind?

– No. I mean, not directly. This is about Billy—or, more precisely, it's not really about Billy except where he tried to insert himself. It's about Ricardo San Roman's much younger daughter, Lorena, who has been, at the least, kidnapped. Maybe on the way to being trafficked out of the country or killed.

– Are you sure she isn't just having fun? Playing for a bit of excitement?

– This young woman is –

She cut me off.

– When they have that much money, you know, they're never really the victim.You have to –

This time I cut her off.

– I'm pretty sure Billy is with her.

– Well, you can imagine how little I care for most of the San Roman clan. But how did Billy get involved?

– Lorena crossed a drug cartel because ... well, for reasons. They didn't appreciate it. Eventually their guys rounded her up and also grabbed Ricardo San Roman. He turned out to be too hot even for them, so they cut him loose. But when they took him, they also grabbed Billy and one of his goons—busy torturing Ricardo at the time.

She giggled. It was the first time I'd seen a positive expression on her face.

– If I were not an officer of the court, I'd like to have been present for that.

– I bet.

– But of course my duty... Wait, what exactly do you want?

– Jeff Spencer thought you might have a way to ... locate Billy. He said you have often proven very effective counsel by knowing precisely where he would be.

I could have been nastier and wanted to be. But this wasn't the time.

– Suppose I could find him. How do I know you don't get the cops involved?

– The cops are already involved. FBI too: Lorena's a minor. It's a bit of a situation, as I'm sure you can imagine. The only thing I can promise is that I won't mention you or Billy if I have to share location info. Assuming we're lucky, they'll all walk out alive. That's two of yours and just one of mine, if we're keeping count.

Carrie was clearly unhappy with what she knew she would have to do. She looked up the street, toward MLK, then back down, sighed, and pulled out her phone.

– Yeah, I have a location feed on him...

She swiped and tapped a bit.

– He's offline now. Maybe no signal. Maybe the phone is dead. But, like I said, he gives me a feed and I have an app to collect the tracks. Let me block all of the earlier waypoints. They're none of anyone's business.

She winked in an offensive manner but showed me the phone screen.

– Here's the track out of town yesterday. Eventually goes out 26, toward the mountain, a bit past Zigzag, then off into the woods, backtracks a bit. Ends here. I'll send you the coordinates.

– Wait, can you send me the whole track—I mean the whole track heading out of town, along with the timestamps? Maybe they stopped somewhere. Maybe there's other info I can use.

She thought for a moment.

– Fine. One sec.

More tapping and swiping.

– You should have it now. You find Billy, you do not have permission to interview him. If he has any sense, he won't talk to anyone. Feel free to tell him that much.

Despite her shoddy legal education and sloppy subsequent work, I was pretty sure she knew her prohibition couldn't stop Billy and me from conversing. I was less sure she realized I wasn't going to give him anything more nor less than the physical, life-saving help he might need. It didn't matter: it was time to end this confab, get to looking at the data, and, it appeared, get on the road to the mountain.

– Thank you, Carrie!

I called out as sincerely as I was able, as I turned back toward MLK, Grand, and the garage and began briskly walking. She said nothing. I glanced back for just a moment and she was already in conference with her gaggle of clients, re-emerged from their burrows.

Before entering the parking garage, I looked at my phone to ensure the data was there and see what flavor it was in. It was present and in a format easy to work with and analyze. I'd need a computer for that, though. Time wouldn't allow me a return to my office. The Belmont library wasn't great but would have to do. I got the Mustang out of the garage and started rolling through the traffic on Hawthorne, hitting mostly red lights. A restaurant reminded me of Paul's last meal with me at Clyde's. A thrift store reminded me of Lorena's teen attempts at Portland punk, not unsuccessful. These memory jogs weren't of the useful sort—there was too much sentiment and not enough insight. They took over my mind anyway.

38

I parked in the little lot behind the Belmont branch next to the metal drop box which—bold letters warned—was *not* a library book drop, but rather a drop for needles and other biohazards. Entering, I cursed the unusable bathrooms. Safe, functioning public bathrooms were always the first victim of general disorder. Happily, the rest of the library branch hadn't suffered so much and still held its charm. It was a cute brick building in a colonial style that wouldn't have been out of place in any small town in New England. The contents—structurally anyway—are what you might have expected in the small town library as well. It worked.

I grabbed a computer at a table near the windows and dove straight into a quick analysis of the GPS data. The file was basically a list of latitude-longitude coordinates, along with elevation and timestamp for each. A track in space and time. Sometimes these files contained extra info—things like the temperature, or the heart rate picked up from a fitness band—which could be useful here ... but no luck. Either the data had never been there, or it had been scrubbed.

The basic track was east toward Mt. Hood, ending in the woods near Zigzag. A solid, functional choice for a hideout but, with a track like the one I now possessed, trivial to find with any GPS or even a phone, assuming you got it all synced up before you lost service in the woods.

There were, however, a couple of kinks in the path both spatially and temporally. It looked like they stopped at the Fred Meyers supermarket-cum-department store in Sandy. But then they also made a stop at a similar Northwest Merchandise store barely half a mile away. That was odd.

Fred Meyer had pioneered modern "one-stop shopping" in Portland's Hollywood neighborhood, creating something like a giant modernized general store, about a hundred years back and decades before the Waltons produced their outsized American icon. Northwest Merchandise, another regional chain, sprang from a common philosophical ancestor but operated with smaller stores and lower prices. Northwest didn't have much that you wouldn't find even more of at Fred Meyer except ... guns and ammo. It wasn't a pleasant thought, but I'd make a quick stop at both places to ask some questions and hopefully find out.

Within fifteen minutes of entering the library, I was back in my car and headed north on Cesar Chavez.

The least painful route—especially this time of day—was I-84 to Troutdale and then south to pick up 26. I got off at the exit before the airport where Paul had made his final takeoff: the one that never gets a matching landing in any logbook.

The city gave way to rural Clackamas County within two minutes, an urban-rural transition that places like Atlanta stretch to an hour and a half. I said a silent prayer to the gods of the growth boundary and let the V8 out a bit.

39

Less than ten minutes later, I wheeled into the parking lot at the Sandy Fred Meyer and saw there was already a message on my phone from Jeff. The family had figured out by now that Lorena—not Paul—had probably attacked Ara with the bottle. The realization gave them an even better reason to get resources into finding her. But they still had no idea where to start.

If she was with Billy, then I had at least half an idea thanks to Carrie, and I told Jeff that much. In his line of work, he more than understood the delicate positions I was frequently in. When I told him I'd share details if and when we needed the cavalry, he sent back a shrug emoji.

The team inside the store was less than informative. They hadn't seen anything unusual. They couldn't let me look at security footage unless we invited the Sandy cops over and the cops agreed that my story warranted the necessary phone calls and corporate paperwork. Even if that all worked out, I didn't expect to learn much from such an exercise. I already knew the crew carrying Billy had been here. I even parked near the same spot they had used (and looked around on the ground for evidence).

I bailed and cruised up the block to try my luck at the Northwest Merchandise, whose cashiers were quite a bit more forthcoming. They related that a guy in tactical garb had picked up a thousand rounds of target plus another dozen boxes of defense ammo. One elderly cashier enthusiastically showed me how she could find the exact time of the purchase on the register screen. It matched the time I had from the GPS track. The clothing and the quantity of ammunition didn't raise any red flags in this locale, but the cashier also noted that the shopper appeared new to the NW Merch experience. Upon arriving, he came in without a membership card, seemed confused about the concept at first, then went in and out to his vehicle twice before showing up with a card belonging to "the wife."

Before leaving the parking lot, I checked the bag in my trunk to make sure my lightweight armor was in there. At least everything the guy had bought was 9mm.

40

Highway 26 was largely empty as I got farther out into the woods, where the road parallels the Sandy River flowing down off the mountain and where the old Barlow Road still winds through the woods alongside both river and highway. From time to time, a truck would come roaring past going the opposite direction, both of us doing about seventy.

One of those times, I got unlucky.

In an instant, a horrific cracking exploded in my face and my view was almost completely occluded by the aquamarine safety glass crater formed in my windshield.

A rock, probably, of some not entirely insignificant size, had come off or been thrown by the passing truck. I checked my rearview mirror and then braked aggressively and pulled off the road. I got out and looked the Mustang over. There was some luck to this after all. Aside from the demolished windshield, there was no other obvious damage. Still, I couldn't drive it. I told myself to be thankful the rock was small enough not to penetrate. And to be thankful I wasn't up on the more exposed part of the mountain.

I looked on my phone to see exactly where I was and to plan my next move. Less than two miles farther up the road,

I'd be near tons of vacation rentals, a camp ground or two, and some businesses. There was no point calling for help or waiting here. I grabbed my bag from the trunk—a handful of essential gear in addition to clothes and the armor—put on my hat and started hoofing it up the grade to the east.

Leaning into the gentle climb, I made it to the minimal mountain town in about fifteen minutes. Clouds were swirling and turbulent around the peak, a few drops of rain blowing down here at the base. I had my pick of sheds that served as vacation resort offices, campground offices, a church ... or a bar and grill. The last reminded me that I had guzzled coffee at Jeff's office but hadn't eaten a thing all day. The Lo Pass was an unimproved roadhouse that appeared to skew more local than tourist. I imagined a passable bite and decent odds of getting a ride farther up the hill without a lot of prying questions.

There were a number of reasons I didn't want questions or the constabulary involved, at least not yet. A big one was that I was more interested in getting Lorena out alive than in catching the bad guys. Billy I could take or leave. But, in any case, my goals meant different tactics.

When I swung open the flimsy door to the Lo Pass, I could tell right away the place was going to deliver. Random "for sale" and "item wanted" postings were stuck on shoulder-high rough-edged drywall meant to partition a small casino corner from the main dining room and bar. A chunky older man smoking a cigarillo sat in that corner and glanced at me momentarily, then back to the flashing of the state lottery game machines. The floor was carpeted for reasons I couldn't imagine. It must have been hell to clean after a raucous night. A foam-panel drop ceiling hovered just above my head.

Four humans and a dog sat at the rounded Formica bar. A large TV showing Cactus League ball hung on a fake-wood-paneled wall. Behind the bar was a cute late-twenties brunette. She and a tourist couple in a booth over toward the highway side of the place looked like they had some life in front of them. The others weren't old but they weren't being treated well by middle age either.

As I sat down at the bar, the brunette asked if I wanted a menu.

I called out my order.

– I'll just have a cheeseburger ... onion rings. Does that work?

– Sure thing. You want something to drink?

From my high stool, I took in the options: in addition to half a dozen tap beers, the shelf of brand name booze and case of God-knows-what in the well, I could see more options through glass panels in six old-fashioned, wood-framed doors on the side of a walk-in cooler. Beer, cider, hard seltzer, a few other things. But the greasy burger would dull my wits as far as I could risk.

– Just a soda water. Thanks.

Leaning back, and looking around the place a bit more, I noticed the door to the men's room hanging open and partly off its hinges. A door closer, of the sort intended for residential screen doors and not commercial bathrooms, hung down off the door frame, connected to nothing.

Something clicked in my memory: taken together, this whole outfit reminded me of finished basements from the 1970s and 1980s where I had spent a lot of time in my youth. They were all kitted out like bars somehow, and shabbily. They provided great playrooms when the grownups weren't putting them to drunken use and, also, sometimes, when they were. In fact, I thought to myself, I'd almost lay the odds this place was converted with a visibly limited effort from a 1970s dwelling.

I listened to the conversation for another minute and my soda arrived. The fellow on my left was quiet but the man and the two women on my right—with the dog—were chatting off and on. The man on my right ordered another Coors Light and began a half-hearted apology for his consumption. His blood pressure was out of control, he was trying to cut down and it wasn't going well.

The woman down the bar to his right explained that her dietary habits weren't contributing to her health either.

– I'm a beige girl... You know, the beige food thing? It's all I've been eating lately.

And the woman to her right—on the end, with the dog—said her gallbladder was failing. She got a couple of looks and had to launch into a short, well worn explanation of what a gallbladder was for and what happened when it was failing. By the time she finished, my cheeseburger and onion rings had landed in front of me.

The motion attracted her attention and synced with the point she was trying to make. She pointed at the onion rings.

– Like that. I love onion rings but I can't hardly digest them. I get all kinds of stomach trouble, especially if I eat them before bed.

Coors Light chimed in:

– Well, just don't eat them before bed.

Before gallbladder, who appeared sad and exasperated by the discussion, started to explain, I jumped in. By coincidence, there had been a gallbladder incident in my family so I knew just enough to empathize effectively.

– Yeah, my brother's gallbladder failed when he was driving back from school one time. He said the pain was unbelievable. Ended up on the side of the road calling 911. Passed out. Woke up in the hospital, they had to take it out. It had burst or something.

Maybe I had gone too far.

– Oh, yeah, sorry. Oversharing? I just mean I understand, you gotta take care of that before it gets too bad.

That got me involved in the chit chat and, a few minutes later, I mentioned my broken windshield. The beer and blood pressure guy offered to get me a tow, but I explained that I wasn't so worried about that—I'd take care of it later—I just needed to get a couple miles farther up the road today.

I was trying, I lied, to get to my buddy's cabin. I could hike in on the gravel road but that was about four more miles away.

Beer man said he'd drive me—and introduced himself as Steve. He needed to get himself off the barstool anyway before he was tempted to order anything else, he said. He and the women, who clearly all knew each other, said their goodbyes. I insisted on covering Steve's pretty minimal bill and he walked me out and pointed to a black Bronco.

For a minute or two, as we drove into the gathering gloom below Mt. Hood, Steve talked about his attempts to stop drinking. He started, he said, by trying to cut down on beer. That didn't work so he tried cold turkey. Also didn't work. Gave up for a while but was back on trying to cut down. The missus was trying to help but he couldn't help sneaking one at the Lo Pass before heading home.

I pointed out a numbered National Forest road and Steve slowed to a stop and let me out. I wasn't completely sure this was the right one. I had just been surreptitiously following the GPS waypoints on my phone while Steve narrated his alcoholic struggles.

I waved and smiled and Steve disappeared up the highway. Fifty meters down the gravel road into the woods, I put on the body armor and a jacket and sat down to plan the crucial next steps.

It was getting toward dusk and I figured low light would work to my advantage. I relaxed a little bit, checked all of my gear, and let the cheeseburger digest for another half hour. The onion rings I had largely left on my plate at the Lo Pass, earning some friendly mockery from the gallbladder patient.

41

I knew where the blue dot ended up on the GPS track, but, since it was in the woods, I had no idea exactly what else was at that location. Ignorance of the area put me at a disadvantage—that and the facts that I was outnumbered, outgunned, and dealing with experienced killers.

Reconnaissance would have to come first. I'd get to the end of the track, see exactly what and maybe even who was there, and, if things worked out, I'd return to my current location and draw a map or a detailed plan.

Throwing on a camo jacket, pants, and hat, I stashed the backpack and started padding along the gravel road. About 500 yards farther, a narrower road—part gravel, part mud—split off and went in a more densely wooded and remote direction. Another 500 yards, and the GPS track left this road as well and went down a wide dirt trail which led to a cluster of buildings.

I left the wide driveway track and found a path through the brush which roughly paralleled it towards the buildings. The driveway appeared to lead to the largest building—itself not terribly large, maybe thirty by twenty-five feet—and then on to a larger area devoid of trees. Behind the largest building, which I assumed had been the main cabin or house, there was an isolated smaller building to the south and east, another to the south and west, and two much smaller buildings—outhouses or sheds—farther still to the west. External lights were on at the main house, but everything else was dim and getting darker. There was no sign of any humans. Tire tracks indicated at least one vehicle had been here at some point, but no vehicle was visible.

The GPS track ended approximately where I was, about forty feet north of the main building.

Staying east of the main house, I crept, close to the ground. I saw nothing but forest. South of the whole complex, the ground dipped and I could hear, and then see, running water: a small creek. On the opposite side of the creek, the ground rose steeply to just above the level of the ground on which I had entered the area.

A few droplets of rain started to come down through the trees.

All of the buildings had just one story and windows on at least two sides, so it would be possible to see inside once it got a bit darker, assuming any building occupants turned on lights and didn't have hotel-grade blackout shades.

Since I had received no indication of anyone or anything thus far, I took the opportunity to circle the entire compound. Typical "mountain shack" setup. Electricity came in the way I had—I could see the lines in the trees. Gas was in an above-ground tank. Water and sewer were, presumably, handled in a more primitive manner.

Although we were less than three miles, as the crow flies, from Route 26, no cell service reached the area due to the surrounding topography.

I took pictures and sketched a primitive map while I could see everything. I even used a rangefinder to check my intuition on distances. Then I turned around the way I came and headed back.

42

A half hour later, it was much darker, due as much to the canyon shadows as to the time of day. The rain was dripping steadily. I got all of my gear together and swapped camo for black.

Once again, I headed down the road to the compound in the forest. I was gambling the outcome of the whole affair on being able to handle whatever happened next.

This time, a lamp was on inside the main cabin and, despite a bit of light pollution from an exterior flood pointing off to my right, I got a good look inside through the binoculars. It was furnished in semi-modern rustic Oregon. Might even be an AirBnB or the like. Some shadows were visible inside but no people. The windows were on the north and east side of the building, the door on the west side. So the move was to breach the door gun drawn, hope for surprise, and figure out the rest when it happened.

I circled the building clockwise. This let me scout the surrounding area in case anything had changed. It also meant I'd avoid the floodlight.

As I passed south of the house, I descended partway into the creek bed to keep a bit more distance between the building and me, as well as to obtain slightly better cover.

I could see more lights on inside through the south-facing window, but still no humans.

Moving closely along the wall of the building, I approached the door. It was classic cabin construction, meant to keep raccoons and skunks out more than people, and I spun and knocked it clear off its hinges with one well placed kick.

Entering the room, I began the sort of half-assed room clearing operation you get from half-assed once-every-two-years training. Then I progressed to the next room and the next. Four and a bath all together. The place was empty, I had made a bit of a racket entering, and now I was the one in the sole illuminated building. At this realization, I dropped to the floor, prepared for shots to ring out. None came.

Not wanting to walk out the front door, I climbed out the bathroom window and dropped to the ground on the east side of the house and waited, then slowly made my way toward the creek.

The rain was falling harder now and it was fairly dark. If someone wasn't already watching me, I could probably move around freely.

I headed west toward the next largest building. Walking in the calf-deep water, I got as close as I could while maintaining cover. The steep, loose slope up from the creek meant that approaching the building was all-or-nothing—no place to stop or spy. If I wanted a look in without sticking myself to the wall and window, I'd need to go up the opposite bank instead. Which I did.

The slightly higher terrain there allowed me to look across the creek, through the window, and into the now-brightly-lit one-room cabin.

This cabin was crowded.

43

Four figures were seated in a row in simple chairs: Weatherson, Lorena, Billy, and Billy's associate. They all faced south across the middle of the room and their arms were all back behind them—likely fastened that way. Billy and his pal were stripped to the waist, wearing just black pants and boots now. Weatherson and the girl still had all their clothes—either they looked less risky or the crooks had some limited sense of decency.

In the southeast corner of the room, light—and presumably heat—was coming off a waist-high kerosene heater. I was momentarily jealous of the comfort as the temp outside was in the forties now and I could see my breath.

I became less jealous as I took in the southwest corner of the room. There, I saw one of the cartel tac ops guys casually keeping watch over the scene. Probably one of the guys who had busted in on Billy, his buddy, San Roman, and me by the boat ramp. He held a vape pen in his left hand while his right rested on a semiautomatic in a drop-thigh holster. A carbine in a sling hung off his shoulder. He looked bored and tired. The nonchalance reminded me of Italian cops I had encountered armed with submachine guns, cigarettes, and absent looks.

The prisoners were engaged in animated conversation. I never could read lips but the talk seemed to involve all four of them.

Occasionally, they'd glance at the guard and say something. Eventually, he started smirking and throwing in a word from time to time but he never got off the wall where he leaned.

I sat and watched as the interaction slowly became more heated. It was clear that Billy, his lieutenant, and Lorena were yelling hostilities now. Some at each other; some at the cartel guard. The doctor seemed to alternate between throwing in a word of his own on the one hand and trying to calm things down on the other.

This dynamic proceeded and escalated for another few minutes when Billy's associate started moving. He was struggling, trying to stand up but failing to do so as it appeared his feet were attached to each other or to the chair legs.

He was screaming something and spitting in the direction of the guard, hopping and jerking his chair, when the guard raised his pistol and I finally heard something over the noise of the rain and the creek and through the sound-dampening glazing in the cabin window: a sharp crack as he casually shot his chair-bound antagonist.

Blood sprayed out onto the wall. But it wasn't a headshot and the boy was still moving vigorously, a look of disbelief on his face. The guard stepped toward him, hit him hard in the face, unfastened his hands and feet, grabbed him under the armpits, and pulled him out of my view.

A moment later, a door in the north side of the cabin opened. In silhouette, the operator emerged from the cabin dragging a man who must have been Billy's lieutenant. The guard heaved and then pushed the wounded prisoner toward the slope and down toward the creek. Then he turned around, entered the cabin, and slammed the door.

The guard reappeared opposite three seated prisoners in the lit room. Without taking his eyes off of them, he slowly dropped the magazine from his pistol, pulled a new one from somewhere on his outfit, and inserted it. He slammed it home and stuck the gun back in the thigh holster, looking as cool and bored as he had before.

44

I scrambled down toward the creek and called out, trying to get the injured man's attention while keeping my volume to a minimum. He either couldn't hear me over the rain and the creek or chose to ignore me—perhaps imagining me a threat—and struggled to pull himself up the bank toward the cabin.

He was clearly seriously hurt: he didn't even make it halfway up the bank.

I came across the creek, still calling to him, a little bit louder now. He kept pulling and dragging himself up the mud and roots. I was below him and climbing.

– I can help you. Stay down here and I'll get you out of here.

He ignored me and finally disappeared over the top with me a few seconds behind.

I got my head above the edge of the bank just in time to see two flashes in the darkness ahead. Billy's friend, crawling away on hands and knees across the open space north of the cabin, collapsed to the ground. He didn't move at all now. I took a few seconds to convince myself of what was happening. Sometime in there I had heard the crack of at least two shots but I wasn't sure when. Everything was still and dark now.

Unless the first guard had gotten out and moved fifty yards away into the woods in the time it took me to scramble across the creek, it wasn't the same guy: there was a second cartel operator moving around outside.

I moved toward the motionless body thinking he might still be alive. As I got my hand on his wrist, another two muzzle flashes, cracks, and bullets hit the ground next to me. I dropped flat, drew, and fired back at the source. I saw a silhouette emerge from the tree line—the gunman was barely fifteen yards away. I fired again twice and connected. The man dropped and didn't move. Neither did a pulse in the wrist I was holding.

I watched the scene—everything motionless except for rivulets of water carving their way through the mud and gravel—as I slowly backed away and retreated down the bank. Both men still lay as they fell when I had reascended the opposite side of the creek and could again see them.

Inside the cabin, the three remaining prisoners appeared agitated. Their custodian, calm as ever, again rested his right hand on the grip of his pistol. But he had set down the vape pen. Instead he held a walkie-talkie in his left hand and was conversing over the device.

I squinted through my binoculars to ensure that it was in fact a walkie-talkie and not some kind of satellite phone, and confirmed my initial impression had been correct. Just a basic radio. Which meant there was at least one other player nearby and possibly more.

While I planned my move against the building and reloaded, I noticed Billy and Lorena talking. They seemed on neutral terms, friendly even. Billy occasionally yelled something in the direction of the guard. The kid had more balls than I would have credited him. Lorena was rocking and scooting her chair a little at a time south and east.

She had migrated most of the way across the room when I decided it was go time.

It was pitch black now outside. I crossed the stream and stepped up the bank toward the window through which I had been watching the action. Then around the corner to my right, one step toward the door. I was preparing to draw my weapon and take the final step to the door when I felt a pain and shock in my chest like a kick from a horse. I flew backward a couple of feet and fell just over the edge of the embankment. Luckily, I landed on the diagonal, so I neither rolled nor slid farther down.

I hopped right back up, which I can only explain by imagining that adrenaline must have dulled the pain from the two 9mm slugs I had taken to the torso. I'm no superman: the body armor saved me from a lethal dose of lead. Later, when the doctors looked at me, they weren't sure I had the sequence of events right given the broken ribs, bruised sternum, some lung damage ... and what happened next.

My battered chest was evidence that on the other end of the walkie talkie was at least one gun and probably a thermal sight. I hesitated at the top of the embankment. It wasn't just that I didn't want to risk another round or two. My fear was that there was a rifle to go along with that sight. Th armor wouldn't help against a rifle: I'd be toast and they'd find my body in the creek if I made for the door.

I stood against the wall of the building, panting and trying to think, when events got ahead of my contemplation. A muffled scream came through the window and I slid my eye over to peek through just in time to see fire—from the kerosene heater Lorena had now kicked over—roar up the southern wall of the cabin, across the floor where fuel had spilled, and up a table covering.

Lorena might have seen my face momentarily at the window—she was looking my way with a grin as I ducked and slid. About a second later, that window shattered and glass shards rained down where I had been.

The whole cabin was blazing now. There must have been some other accelerant—a propane tank or a gas line—somewhere. I lifted my head above the edge of the bank and saw a figure silhouetted by firelight emerge from the front door of the cabin, trousers burning.

It turned toward me—I saw the face and bare torso: it was Billy. A shot rang out, catching him from behind. He stepped and fell face-first toward me.

I grabbed him, rolled him to extinguish the flames from his pants, and pulled him down to cover in the creek bed. He was moaning and looked me in the eye.

– Man! I fucked this all up. I don't know… I don't know what I was thinking. I can't breathe. It hurts so much.

I started by reassuring him.

– It's not that bad. Barely got you. You'll just be a bit sore.

A quick exam suggested I was being optimistic but not absurdly so. He was hit pretty good and bleeding decently, but he could breathe. The bullet hadn't hit arteries or pierced a lung.

I thought about his buddy, the one who was already gone, and wondered why Billy deserved to skate out of the shit again. But I quickly pushed the thought away—there would be time enough for that if we all made it out. For now, I rummaged through my first aid supplies for a bleed stop packet and some gauze, jammed it on the wound where it quickly did its job, wrapped the chest with tape to get more pressure on it, and looked around.

To the north, reflecting off the low clouds and refracting in the fog, were dim, oscillating red and blue lights. The cavalry was in the vicinity, probably half a mile away through the woods.

Crackling and loud boot steps on gravel came from the top of the embankment.

I looked at Billy and pointed east, where the lights were.

– Here's your best bet: stay down in the creek and crawl as fast as you can in that direction. I'll distract these guys. There'll be –

I cut myself off: I thought of the impending irony when Billy would emerge from the woods, crawling up to the feet of the sheriff's deputies, begging for help. I had better rephrase.

– There's a … an ambulance there. Go!

I wasn't sure there'd be any ambulance yet.

Billy turned and started crawling up the stream. I saw a light above me at the top of the creek and I started firing steadily toward it but into the trees. I was trying to provide cover for Billy as he dragged himself away in the water and mud while at the same time ensuring I didn't hit someone I hadn't yet identified. Billy made it underneath some bushes and other growth overhanging the creek and I started climbing—for the third time? fourth time?—up to the cabin, now entirely ablaze.

I scrambled to my left, around the flames and the cabin, so that when I needed to reload, I wouldn't be at the same spot where Billy and I had gone down. No one met me at the top of my scramble.

Looking around, I circled the fire-engulfed building clockwise. Around the third corner, I saw the same guard who had been inside. He stood in the gravel near where the cabin's door had once been.

He was holding Lorena's arm in one hand and Weatherson's wrist in the other. Weatherson was on the ground kneeling. Lorena struggled in the man's grip, twisting: her feet were still shackled. The man turned and looked right at me. I raised my weapon. Lorena was in between my gun and her captor. She coughed and fell forward, bending at the waist. That provided an opening. I fired three times, with the third shot removing the top half of the man's head.

Lorena dropped to the ground coughing. The doc was on his knees sobbing like a baby.

46

I picked up Lorena, threw her over my shoulder in a fireman's carry, and yelled at Weatherson.

– Get the hell up! There's help half a mile away but we gotta get there.

He just sort of looked at me and whimpered. I kicked him in the thigh, hard. That seemed to snap him back to reality. He stopped blubbering and stumbled to his feet. Unlike Lorena, his hands and feet were all free. He could move under his own power if he were in the mood to do so.

I took a step toward the gravel path that led out of the compound and looked back at him. He stood up.

I took another step.

– Come on, man. Get your shit together.

I took another step and this time he followed me. We were making progress. To generate some extra motivation—both for him and for myself—I vocalized my biggest concern.

– You know, there's at least one more guy in the woods here, well fucking armed. There might be more.

The doc looked like he was about to say something when, on cue, that third man emerged from the wood line in front of us. He had a rifle with a light pointed at us, just fifty feet away.

But he didn't fire. It could only be Lorena and Weatherson that made the difference. If they weren't toast by now, maybe that was because he needed them alive. With Lorena draped over me, he couldn't take a shot. I had one hand free and squeezed off two shots at him.

The light winked out. He was gone.

Weatherson had seized up again. I kicked him again.

– Let's go!

We marched out, up the path toward the wider gravel road, the hissing and crackling of the burning building behind us mixing with the white noise of the streaming rain. The woods were dense and soon we were beyond the radius of the building's light.

We had just about reached the gravel road and I was starting to think about the statement I'd need to make to the cops and about the beers that would follow.

Things didn't quite work out that way.

47

Boots crunched the earth behind me. As I slowly turned, the inertial moment of Lorena's mass limiting my agility, I saw Weatherson turn a much quicker one-eighty, just in time to get a large knife straight to the gut from our black-clad friend.

He had circled around and gotten behind us. He'd almost made it on top of us when his footsteps gave him away. He withdrew the tactical blade from the doctor's gut and the ensuing rush of blood spelled doom for a man who was far from pure but hardly deserved this ending.

I didn't even have the luxury of speaking to him as he collapsed: the man in black whirled toward me with the knife.

Now, I'm ok with a gun. And I've been shot with and without armor before. But fighting a trained operator with a knife is just about my worst nightmare. I barely had enough training to disarm a slow drunk and was way out of practice for even that much of a challenge. I was about to get myself filleted.

Instinctively, I dropped Lorena to the ground and moved to parry and get inside the knife. I made it most of the way as the blade nicked my hip. Lorena scratched and scrambled away toward the edge of the road. The forearm holding the knife was in front of my face and I bit it hard. Like all the way. The knife dropped. I threw an elbow. A grunt and wheeze. And again, feeling the soft crack of a rib. I just might have a chance, I thought.

Lorena gave a shriek. She was struggling along the edge of the road valiantly despite her chains, when a root or rock caught a foot. Unable to recover her balance with feet bound, she went down sharply right into a broken stump.

My head got yanked away from that sight by a very muscular arm tightening into a chokehold on my throat. A hand methodically and smoothly stripped and discarded my gun, backpack, light, and multitool. My neck was immobilized; I couldn't twist out at all. I let my knees go and as my weight collapsed directly earthward my attacker's grip weakened. I was on the ground and he maneuvered above me.

Groping the ground, I got hold of a rock. It was small, but had some mass and jagged edges. I went for speed and hit the side of the man's head. Didn't make it. He grabbed the arm and his other hand appeared with another blade. At least this knife was smaller than the first.

He wrestled and slashed. We were both tiring or he would have gotten me. The dance continued several more steps before his training overcame my lack of it and he slashed my deltoid. The pain stunned me and in an instant I was face down in the dirt. Something metal cracked across the back of my head and I felt my consciousness slipping away. Before everything went black, however, the man's weight shifted. Somehow I could think a little bit. I rolled to my side, drawing my boot up to my buttocks.

From my boot, I managed to pull my last hope: a practically microscopic North American Arms .22 Magnum revolver. The man's left arm went up with the knife as he prepared for the kill. Before he brought the blade down, I jammed the roughly inch-long barrel of the revolver into the soft armpit above the side panel of his body armor, thumbed the hammer, and fired a WMR slug sideways into his heart. Just in case, I thumbed and fired a second time.

I rolled him off of me and looked for Lorena.

48

I found her just off the edge of the road, sore, stunned, wide-eyed, silently staring at the man I had just killed.

She probably didn't even know who that was.

– Do you recognize him?

– Uhh. No. Should I?

– Does the name Magenta mean anything to you?

– No, I... Wait, I think I heard dad and Ara talking about her a long time ago...

– Magenta is a "he" and, well, that's him over there.

I gestured.

She looked at me quizzically.

– Don't worry about it, I'll explain later.

– What about the doctor?

She struggled to get over to where Weatherson lay in a large muddy pool of his own blood.

– He's gone.

Lorena, shell-shocked up to that point or maintaining an extraordinary stoic facade, suddenly began sobbing. Wailing. Trying to get close to him.

Confusion showed on my face when I gently pulled her away.

She looked at me through the tears.

– He's the only one... The only... The... He helped. Helped Paul. He saved him. Paul has a chance now because of him and...

Suddenly I realized: she didn't know about Paul. Well, I sure as hell wasn't going to force her to deal with that tonight. I just nodded and picked her back up in the fireman's carry. She yelped: the recent fall had done some damage. I shifted her weight and my balance and set off up the narrow road. A bit later we got to the forest road and quickly after that the turnoff from US 26.

The place was lit up like Christmas: two sheriff SUVs, an ambulance, a National Forest ranger truck, and a Hoodland Fire District truck. Billy was visible in the ambulance. A black-clad operator was cuffed and seated on the ground. An EMT with bolt cutters freed Lorena's ankles.

Taking one of the Clackamas County deputies aside, I arranged to put off the interviews and statements until the following day. He offered to drive Lorena and me back to the city: to the hospital or home. We both opted for the latter.

It was a long quiet ride broken occasionally by radio traffic.

We were crossing the river when I spoke to Lorena.

– I have some solid ideas for cleaning things up so you can think about living at home and doing normal teenage stuff. But we have to send back the rest of the money...

– I know. Paul was right all along... The crypto info and everything is in my laptop. My dad can get it for you. But he doesn't have the password. It's "coffee4ever." Like with the number four.

Despite the somber mood, the deputy driving us couldn't suppress a chuckle: coffee almost edged out beer among local religious affiliations and among the addictions less likely to land you in a tent.

– Oh. No. Actually... Coffee was my cat. When I was a kid. See, she wasn't black, she was dark brown everywhere. She was actually pretty special. She... Never mind. It's a long story.

The deputy dropped me outside my apartment building and pulled away with Lorena, bound for her mom's house—Carolina's house. Lorena's face was up against the window of the cruiser, watching me. Tears were flowing.

49

The next day, after four grueling hours of police interviews, I rented a car, since mine was still on the mountain needing a tow and a windshield. I drove I-84 back out toward Troutdale Airport but took a right instead of a left at the bottom of the exit ramp. At the shelter, there was exactly one all-brown kitten and she was a beauty.

When I got to Carolina's house, it was all locked up, no one around. At San Roman's house, I sat with Ricardo, who was in a hospital bed in a solarium at the back of the property. He was covered in a lot of bandages but he was lucid. His eyes went wide at the sight of the kitten. He took a deep breath and let it out. I nodded. He spoke softly.

– Take good care of it.

– What do you mean? This is for –

– Lorena isn't going to be back for a long while... Carolina took her to stay with a cousin in California.

I stroked the cat and pointed with my eyes.

– Maybe... You...?

He shook his head and murmured something. Settled his head into the pillow and closed his eyes.

I looked around. We were alone. And I had a cat.

9 798999 181160 6